As Sheep Among Wolves

Pages from a Vicar's Diary

As Sheep Among Wolves

Pages from a Vicar's Diary

Simon Peterson

ATHENA PRESS
LONDON

As Sheep Among Wolves
Pages from a Vicar's Diary
Copyright © Simon Peterson 2007

All Rights Reserved

No part of this book may be reproduced in any form
by photocopying or by any electronic or mechanical means,
including information storage or retrieval systems,
without permission in writing from both the copyright
owner and the publisher of this book.

ISBN 10-digit: 1 84401 990 X
ISBN 13-digit: 978 1 84401 990 8

First Published 2007 by
ATHENA PRESS
Queen's House, 2 Holly Road
Twickenham TW1 4EG
United Kingdom

Printed for Athena Press

Foreword

I have been asked to write a few words to commend the memoirs of the Reverend Simon Peterson, who was vicar of Chilford in my early days as archdeacon of Bilchester.

This is not an easy task. For, as I see it, the image of the clergy among the secular majority is of a very pale ghost. They may think they are important members of society, but they preach a message that many people just do not want to hear and live uneventful lives that have no interest for the public at large. The best that many vicars can hope for is to be nice, inoffensive men who are in the vicarage if they are wanted. As they seldom are wanted, one has to take or find specialist newspapers or magazines to know much about them or their work.

Those of them who do attract media attention usually appear under one of three headings:

1. They publish something so heretical, even blasphemous, that, even if it delights the thoughtful atheist, shocks normal religious sensibilities.

2. They manage to embezzle church funds.

3. They commit adultery with one of their parishioners.

Even these have somewhat lost their edge through weary repetition in the more sensational newspapers. And a certain couple in the last category had to pose together for the camera with a smirk of self-satisfaction on their faces and publish a long article justifying activities that crippled the proclamation of the gospel, disgraced the Church and betrayed the Lord.

Simon Peterson has never been a partaker in these escapades. He was a conscientious, hard-working and popular parish priest.

Nevertheless, I do owe him something. Shortly before the breakdown that put an end to his ministry in Chilford, I came to the conclusion that he was making a mess of his job and told him so. To my shame, I had been listening to hostile gossip and I repent bitterly.

After all, most of us have religious appreciation and would accept that the Church has a necessary part to play in society. Human characters are interesting, and many faithful souls are trying to make the Church fulfil its purpose.

I warmly commend these memoirs accordingly.

The Venerable Jasper Mackston

2 Cathedral Close,
Bilchester

Contents

1. Is Vicar a Sheep?	9
2. The Desk	11
3. That's Your Job, Vicar	14
4. As a Thief in the Night	17
5. Cedric	20
6. Filthy Lucre	23
7. That Unlovable Woman	25
8. Our Ancient Rights	28
9. The Vicar's Wife	30
10. A Perfect Wife	33
11. The Food of Love	36
12. One of Us	39
13. Mr Demos	42
14. By Their Fruits…	45
15. Inflation	47
16. Public Meeting	50
17. Wolves at the Door	53
18. Retreat	55
19. Bait for the Wolves	58
20. Black Dog	61
21. *Lèse-majesté*	63

22. Sheep, Wolves or Goats?	66
23. Holiday	69
24. A Break with Tradition	72
25. Funeral	75
26. Doom Watch	78
27. A Priest For Ever	81
28. But Nobody…	84
29. Paranoid	87
30. Not too Holy Baptism	90
31. Nothing to Wear	93
32. Vicar's so Broad-minded	96
33. Training the Cubs	99
34. Why so Sad?	102
35. Youth Club	105
36. The Seat of the Scornful	108
37. What am I Worth?	110
38. Isn't it Awful?	112
39. Meet Me Where You Are	115
40. Outing	118
41. PCC	121
42. Remorse	124
43. The Lore and the Profits	127
44. Peace be with You	130
Epilogue	132

1
Is Vicar a Sheep?

1 January 1987

Really, there were occasions when our Lord could be very rude.

For, when he sent his disciples out to do a spot of evangelism, he told them that they were going 'as sheep among wolves'. Presumably he wanted to make them think.

I felt this very much when I accepted the living of Chilford, the place in Barsetshire (I believe there is also one in Devon). I was one of those clergy who think that a parish priest's basic job is to attempt the reconciliation of men (and women) to their Maker – in other words, to evangelise.

When I view those brainless, woolly creatures pottering about the fields with nothing to do but eat and have a haircut and twins once a year, I wonder whether I really appreciate being called a sheep. I have to remember that in the mouth of the Lord it is an expression of loving concern and I must learn to wear it graciously.

On the other hand, it is just a trifle unfair to designate the inhabitants of Chilford a pack of wolves. Many, such as Sue Chamberlain and young Mr James, are among the salt of the earth and love their Lord with a devotion that puts many of us older folk to shame.

Nor, when I do a round of those gentle, loving and devout old ladies, do I ever feel like Red Riding Hood visiting her grandmother.

In my case, I think the Lord was referring to persons such as Mr Worthington and Mr Demos; especially Mr Demos. Even so, to call Mr Demos a wolf is to plaster him with the grossest flattery.

To come down to earth, I quite realise that the Lord is telling us that, when we set out in our youthful enthusiasm to work for his Kingdom of Love, we are going to meet a lot of opposition; much of it subtle, and most of it ignorant.

We had better move on to the next part of the instruction, the small print, as it were. We are told by Matthew to be 'wise as serpents and harmless as doves'.

Does wisdom in this context mean having the ability to sum people up accurately? Jesus himself was an expert but I, for one, have a lot to learn. I am normally far too gullible to see much below the surface; and, even if I do recognise the wolf behind Mr Demos' bullying ways, I am not sure how to deal with the brute.

Perhaps I must be 'harmless as a dove'. Does that mean I must be loving and sympathetic to all men and women, including Mr Demos? Maybe so. It can be a mighty challenge in some cases but I am, alas, duty-bound to make the effort.

Possibly being 'harmless as doves' means avoiding giving offence. This is unlikely in the mouth of Jesus, considering his own record with the Scribes and Pharisees. I am less certain about it.

I find that some of the wolves are all too ready to take offence. For example, when I first came to Chilford, how could I possibly know, unless I was told, that Farmer Gatacre always provided two shocks of corn for the harvest festival?

I was not told; so I begged them, and got them from another farmer. And then, to add insult to injury, Mr Churchwarden Demos, who should have fed me with the necessary information, goes to Farmer Gatacre and says, 'New vicar doesn't want you.'

If being harmless as a dove means treating this sort of unhelpfulness with a gracious smile, this dove has not yet reached maturity. I resent very much this kind of gratuitous opposition, especially from the man who, above all others, should be backing me up in my work. And I don't mind saying so!

There are, of course, a few paranoid wolves who are always on the alert to take offence at anything the vicar says or does.

There are also a few paranoid sheep who are always expecting to be treated in this fashion.

2
The Desk

11 January

Here I sit, as usual on a Saturday morning, 'doing my homework', as Christine calls it. Officially, it is the sacred hour of sermon preparation, the theory being that perusal of tomorrow's Gospel turns on a flood of inspiration that flows gracefully from mind through arms and fingers to the sheet of virgin paper in the typewriter.

As usual, theory is seldom borne out by practice. The mind does indeed collect a few thoughts from the Gospel but they tend to behave in the manner of a rugger scrum and get tangled up with each other until the ball of concentrated thought flies off at a tangent and gets fragmented into other thoughts that have nothing to do with the matter in hand.

Meanwhile, the virgin sheet of A4 in the typewriter remains as pure as the epithet indicates.

My mind strays into a blank, and my eye strays over my desk. It is a magic desk, in that unwanted papers are constantly turning up out of the accumulated mess, while something urgently required, which you know you put down only yesterday, has completely disappeared.

In the early days of our marriage, when we were both young and idealistic, Christine used to make the most praiseworthy efforts to tidy my desk. But, happily, she gave up the struggle before she went completely round the bend. As I explained to her at the time, things left on my desk may disappear temporarily when they are wanted, but if they are put away they vanish for ever.

My eyes wander from the desk to the bookshelves with their numerous volumes shoved in anyhow and to the overspill of books, papers, files, cassettes, videos, wires and odd bits of clothing that litter the floor, and I think how cosy it all is.

I remember the occasion when I had to go to see our archdeacon on some trivial matter. I was shown into his study and kept waiting for a quarter of an hour or so.

The Archdeacon himself is one of those clerical types who go about looking like a Wippell's advertisement, and his study lives up to the image. There is a place for everything and everything is in its place. When I went, the desk was completely clear of clutter and the only things on the floor were things that ought to be on the floor: chairs, waste-paper basket and so on. Even the word processor and the telephone were neatly arranged on their appointed locations and all the day's mail was in the out tray, indicating that it had been dealt with pronto – quite contrary to my practice. And the books, which covered two walls to the ceiling, were meticulously arranged according to subject, author and size.

I pulled one out as I waited. It was entitled *The Parish Priest*, and was the work of a cleric of equal status to my host.

I opened it at random and read the following:

> You can always tell the character of a priest by the state of his desk.

Very well, then! I'm untidy, disorderly and uncoordinated; I waste hours looking for papers that are under my eyes, or testing videos for something I have scrubbed off only yesterday. I am the despair of a good housekeeper and a disgrace as a man of business.

And I don't care – well, not too much anyway – though there is a spiritual entity I call Cedric who inhabits my better nature and tells me that it is not always very kind to others to be so inefficient and mentally airy-fairy.

Against the cosiness of muddle must be set the frustration and angst engendered by continually failing to find what is wanted because it is not placed in an orderly fashion.

And what about the time spent searching? As Cedric takes it

upon himself to remind me sometimes, 'God has not given us too much time to get on with his work.'

Even so, I find him wonderfully patient.

He needs to be, with some of us!

3
That's Your Job, Vicar

18 January

I do wish people would realise what I am here for.

I have just been told by a parishioner that I ought to revise and update the pamphlet on our church's history, which we put up for sale on a table at the back of the church. This good lady never comes to church herself, but she has read books and done some research and has decided that our pamphlet is inaccurate in some respects, has omitted one or two items of historical interest (including mention of the fact that her grandfather was churchwarden for over forty years) and needs updating by some twenty summers.

I suggested that she might do the job herself and the church would do the printing.

'Oh no, Vicar! That's your job.'

In my youth, I played the organ but it is one of those things I was never too keen on and has got crowded out of my life by more important or interesting matters. I have not played for years.

Nevertheless, 'You should give organ recitals, Vicar, and raise money for the church.'

I protest that a recital would entail a lot of practice, which I have not the time for, nor, to be honest, the inclination, to give.

The possibility that, 'properly advertised', it might bring some people to church who do not come on a normal Sunday may be a point in favour. It might make more money, though I doubt it. But, of course, 'It's your job, Vicar, to make money for the church.'

Ugh! If it is my duty to give organ recitals, it is a duty I will delegate with pleasure.

I am reminded of the case of David Sheppard, the Cambridge cricketer who captained England in the fifties. Answering a call to the ministry, he was ordained and eventually had a long and distinguished career as Bishop of Liverpool.

He commenced his career as a curate in London, where he was much engaged in youth work. When the time came for the Test team to go abroad, it was taken for granted by some enthusiasts that David would throw up his work as a clergyman for as long as necessary and captain them.

I was shocked by this. But then, I am not a cricketer and I suppose that I must understand that, in the view of the general public, a clergyman's job is a comfortable little side issue that he may indulge when he has nothing better to do. And obviously sport or politics, say, are much more important than conducting religious services that few people want.

'Don't be so daft and uncharitable,' says Cedric, my conscience, at this point. (He *will* keep pushing his way to the surface). 'You know perfectly well that most people who think at all on such matters realise that your work involves far more than conducting badly attended church services. Do stop moaning!'

Of course. It is my job to visit the sick, in hospital or at home, to organise church business, take care of buildings, furnishing, finance, etc.; to be responsible for the activities of churchwardens, treasurers, cleaners, flower arrangers and so on; to chair the Parochial Church Council (PCC) and conduct meetings, or attend them if conducted by others; to serve on diocesan committees and represent the points of view of my parishioners; to take part in any parish activity and patronise every event; and, overall, to avoid giving offence and to do what my parishioners expect me to do, whether they tell me what that is or not.

And that is a pretty long list, covering a considerable range of activity.

This raises another problem.

There are only some sixteen hours in a working day.

I read that the original purpose of the priesthood was to reconcile sinful men to God. If a priest, then, feels he has to curtail his activities, he might do worse than cut out those things that in no way contribute to such a worthy purpose.

And, maybe, if both he and his parishioners recognise that his job is essentially to promote the love of God by any means, there might be less variety of opinion on the subject.

Cedric can put that in his pipe and chew it over.

4
As a Thief in the Night

25 January

Somewhere, the scriptures warn us that the day of the Lord will come upon us suddenly and unexpectedly. The same evidently applies to the day of Mrs Shorncliff.

Mrs Shorncliff has been the caretaker of our church hall for many years. I inherited her from two or three previous incumbents. Theoretically, she sweeps the place out once a week. And, though I have a key, it is normal for those using the hall to apply to Mrs Shorncliff.

For these services she receives a pittance from church funds. She is a casual churchgoer and is always a 'character'. She holds strong opinions on many subjects, most of them founded on prejudice rather than reason, and we all know that, once crossed, she neither forgets nor forgives. So far, I have never had any trouble with her. As far as I know, the letting of the hall has always gone smoothly. And, with so much else to think about, I have tended to take Mrs Shorncliff and the letting of the hall as a part of normal routine.

Until last month. For then the day of Mrs Shorncliff came as a thief in the night. She rang the vicarage bell and I answered the door. She ignored my invitation to come in and bestowed upon me a grim mouth and the sort of basilisk stare that might have put her in serious danger in witch-hunting days.

'Here are the keys,' she said. 'You can look after your own hall.'

Caught off guard, I goggled at her.

'But— has something gone wrong?' I stammered, a particularly fatuous remark, if ever there was one.

'I'll help anyone,' she said, 'but I'll not be imposed upon.'

And that is all I could get out of her. Off she went, leaving the keys in my hand.

Who 'imposed on her' I do not know to this day. It cannot have been me, because she continues to appear spasmodically at Evensong. And though we are not exactly bosom friends, we are still on speaking terms.

I have met this sort of behaviour once or twice before. Two people suddenly find themselves at war without any ultimatum or declaration of hostilities. Mrs Ascott and Mrs Boscombe are such a pair.

They are both elderly widows and had been friendly for years.

Once a week without fail, Mrs Ascott would pack herself a picnic lunch and go round to Mrs Boscombe. They would have their meal and natter together for a couple of hours or so.

One week, Mrs Ascott turned up as usual. The door was half open, and the face of a belligerent Mrs Boscombe revealed itself.

'And what may you be wanting?' enquired the face.

Mrs Ascott, a meek type, was understandably speechless.

'Well, I don't want you, thank you very much,' said Mrs Boscombe, shutting the door.

In writing this, I would wish that I was just repeating village gossip. But Mrs Boscombe told me the story herself, and she told it with triumph! She explained that she had decided that Mrs Ascott was taking her for granted and she was not one that people might take for granted.

The snubbing of Mrs Ascott, so cruelly done, was a tremendous boost to her little ego. The loss of years of friendship was a worthy price to pay for a day or two of one-upmanship.

And so the cry goes up, 'I don't know what I have done, but so-and-so won't speak to me. If only I knew what was wrong, I could apologise and try to put it right; but I just can't think of anything I might have said to cause offence.'

I find it all rather depressing. These people call themselves Christians ('I'm willing to help anyone, but…'). Some of them are churchgoers, if casual.

Most of us know, and subscribe to, the commandment to love

our neighbours, but too often we seem to add the rider, 'but on my own terms and provided my neighbour continues to take the initiative.'

No wonder the Prince of Peace has such difficulty in reconciling individuals, societies and nations who prefer to go on fighting to the finish.

5
Cedric

1 February

I have always had a conscience of sorts, like most of us; but it is only recently that I have got down to considering his nature.

I say 'him', and I mean 'him'. I know he is a sexless entity like the angels or other spiritual persons, but I refuse to be drawn into any futile arguments with ardent feminists about the gender of the being.

Presumably the desire to personify him has fought its way out of my subconscious, where he may have started materialising following my viewing of Disney's cartoon film *Pinocchio* many years ago.

It will be remembered by Disney fans that Pinocchio's conscience was some species of bug, clad very respectably in morning dress and top hat, who stood on the end of Pinocchio's nose and preached him moral sermons of an improving kind.

My nose is not nearly long enough for this sort of behaviour and even if I could squint sufficiently badly to see someone using it as a pulpit, he would still be badly out of focus.

My conscience does his noble work of exhorting me to virtue from within.

But why do I call him Cedric?

This is a little more difficult to explain. I think my subconscious must have been presenting to my notice the titular character of *Little Lord Fauntleroy*, whose name, if I remember it correctly, was Cedric.

In my youth, Little Lord Fauntleroy was the object of sneering mirth. We mocked! Naturally none of us had read the book but, in an age of violent reaction against anything we could call Victorian, his little lordship was the epitome of all that was sissy, prissy, wet, wimpish, namby-pamby and generally contemptible – completely foreign to the virile, aggressive, macho image we had of ourselves.

It is therefore only right and proper that Cedric, Lord Fauntleroy, has recently appeared in the Disney films. I notice that he has had a much needed haircut, has dispensed with his lace collar and changed his pansy suiting for something more acceptable.

It is an insult to call him 'little'. He seems to be twelve or thirteen, the very best age of pre-adolescent boyhood, and a splendid specimen of the type.

I have no objection to his telling me where to get off sometimes, as the original used to tell his old curmudgeon of a grandfather a century ago.

Nevertheless, conscience is a complex matter, since some examples may be remarkably elastic. I could wish that all consciences could belong to a union, and so, in a way, be under one authority.

This problem has recently been highlighted in the Anglican Church by the issue of women priests. Many persons, clerical and lay, just cannot accept them, and certainly not receive Communion at their hands. And some have left the Anglican community as a consequence.

It is a matter of conscience.

I myself, instinctively against the ordination of women to the priesthood, have prayed about it and examined the issue in the context of biblical study and have come to accept those validly ordained without a twinge of conscience.

I have asked Cedric to explain. Why does he not go along with his counterpart in the soul of the ex-rector of St Anselm's up the road, for example? 'Those women', as he calls them, send his blood pressure soaring dangerously on sight.

'It's like this,' said Cedric. 'I have to share my quarters in your soul with other entities, notably the spirits of Prejudice and Wishful Thinking. Their arguments can be very persuasive and, if we are not careful, influence us consciences unduly. Most wishful thinkers, I find, suffer from a degree of delusion, while the prejudiced need to examine the source of their prejudice. Some sources are a great deal sounder than others.'

'And what do you mean by "sound"?' I asked.

'Firmly built on twin rocks,' he said. 'The spirit of Jesus and the word of God as revealed in the scriptures.'

'Then,' I said, 'please ensure that your sermons to me are so firmly built. It is the only way I can feel secure.'

6
Filthy Lucre

8 February

There were occasions during my early, idealistic days as a young incumbent when, basking in the sunshine of my own piety, I would be suddenly possessed by a devil.

I might wake up to the fact that weddings and funerals earned church fees and that I was pleased to conduct them for that reason. The devil made no excuses for the suggestions. He did not argue that, stipends being what they were in those days, I could do with a few extra pounds. It was simply a matter of the heavier the money bags, the better.

Since those days, the Church's authorities have taken steps to thwart this particular little devil. In their worthy efforts to provide the clergy with a more gracious standard of living, they have clawed a little back by deducting church fees from the vicar's wages.

Even so, there are other channels we may exploit to satisfy our acquisitive instincts. And, in spite of being thwarted on funeral fees, this little devil has grown fat on a number of alternative propositions.

There is, for example, the way of false returns. Taking the famous parable of the unjust steward to heart, and misinterpreting it in the process, I might conduct a dozen funerals in a year and write down six for the eyes and action of the financial authorities. No one will check against the church registers and I would be six funeral fees in pocket. Dishonest? Oh, but vicars are mortal men and everyone does things like that, don't they?

Sometimes one would think so. Once I employed a professional to make out my income tax returns. He probably thought he was doing me a favour by stretching a point here and there. But Cedric was soon on his high horse, telling me that any such fiddles, however small, were very wrong, especially in a clergyman.

I dispensed with professional services and did the job myself. Now, if there are mistakes in my returns, they are at any rate honest ones.

Nevertheless, I have discovered from experience (though possibly a bit late) that when a vicar successfully fights financial temptation on the personal level, the devil may sidestep and deliver a swinging backhander on the vicarious front. I have met, for example, clerical brethren who, though doubtless strictly honest in their own dealings, will sanction false returns to the diocese to reduce their quotas and think they are doing their parishes a favour thereby.

My fat little devil never gives up. He can make hay with the principle that a parish should pay all of a vicar's expenses of office. If we put our minds to it, it is marvellous what we may think up and call expenses of office. And, unless we are much more popular than we deserve to be, a little exaggeration, a little bending of the rules, a little – let's face it – cheating, can render relationships with the church treasurer distinctly unchristian. Personally, I do not find a little greed worth that sort of result.

There is one more temptation that creeps up on us. We may easily join the chorus of self-congratulation and praise of Mammon if fund-raising exercises produce glowing results and that thermometer at the church gate rises by leaps and bounds. It is all very well when it is accompanied by a spiritually healthy congregation rejoicing in the worship of God; but if only two or three are gathered together, and God marginalised, what is really the point of it all?

And with this little bleat of a sheep to the wolves, I must lay down my pen for the time being. My attitude to money may well be regarded as madness in the world of business but it does keep Cedric quiet, and makes for a more comfortable relationship with God.

7

That Unlovable Woman

15 February

Mrs Gullivant is in great distress and I find it difficult to comfort her.

This is not for personal reasons. She has been a regular churchgoer all her life and has always accepted me as her parish priest and respected me accordingly. I should be able to deal with her and I cannot!

The trouble is that Mrs Gullivant is, frankly, a very selfish and not very lovable woman. It has always been so. She was left a widow fairly young, with a teenage daughter to bring up. The two of them have never got on well together, probably because she was a domineering and excessively critical parent who attempted to mould the young life strictly according to her own ideas of what a socially acceptable young lady should be.

Doubtless, the daughter feels a certain dutiful responsibility for the old lady but, even today, any effort made for them to live together would be a recipe for disaster. Mrs Gullivant's critical and domineering faculties have not mellowed appreciably with age.

She married again, a man much younger than herself who was content to play a subsidiary role. It was a case of 'Go, and he goeth. Do this, and he doeth it.' Consequently, she was able to indulge her style of living at the expense of a husband who was little more than a personal servant and errand-boy.

This was not good for her, nor for her reputation. The neighbours regarded her as a self-centred and self-indulgent old woman who did only what she wished to do, while others and her husband were expected to do the rest and to do it up to her exacting standards.

Then Mr Gullivant suffered a crippling stroke, which did not affect his mind, but left him increasingly helpless. He spent about a month in hospital, where he was utterly miserable. He wanted, he said, to die in his own home.

It speaks volumes for our social services that this proved possible. He came home and lived on for some three years; but only with the help of relays of nurses, social workers and neighbours who came, day in, day out, to get him up, put him to bed and attend to him at intervals.

His illness profited Mrs Gullivant considerably because she was now compelled to do much more herself, much of it to serve him. But it would have been helpful if she could have appreciated all that the others were doing. As it was, few of the army of helpers were able to do things to her liking and she did not mind telling them so. The neighbours were regaled with tales of their incompetence and how, if they were a little late arriving, they were 'letting her down'.

I once tried to point out that these were busy people who were properly trained and anxious to provide a helpful service. But Mrs Gullivant would have none of it. She would say that they were paid to do the job, that she had a right to their services and that they should do things properly.

It was not easy to feel sympathy for Mrs Gullivant, and some of us did not try. Those who had known her for a long time said that she had never done anything for anyone else and it served her right if nobody was now anxious to help her.

And then, very mercifully, Mr Gullivant died.

My immediate visit to the widow was not very happy. Perhaps she realised that she would be very lonely. But, whatever the reason, she insisted that he should still be alive. It was only the incompetence and neglect on the part of the medical services that had killed him. She even spoke of the possibility of 'claiming compensation'.

I simply did not know how to cope with this attitude and dreaded my visit after the funeral. But by then she was a little more settled. She said she had now nothing to live for, but was on her way to accepting that his death was merciful and 'God's will'. She was grateful now for all that had been done for him, especially by the neighbours, and asked me to pray with her.

She was broken, and I could feel for her as never before.

Mrs Gullivant had become lovable.

8
Our Ancient Rights

22 February

I have recently returned from a meeting called to settle a little controversy in the parish. It concerns a legacy left to the church many years ago on conditions very reasonable at the time, but quite eccentric under modern conditions.

Around the year 1800 there lived in Chilford a Lady Godolphin. She was a childless widow, whose husband's death had brought about the extinction of the barony. She was something of a Lady Bountiful, who felt she owed a duty to the poor. When she died, the estate was sold off. The manor house is now an old people's home and most of the surrounding land is covered with modern housing.

In her will, she combined her charitable duties to the church and to the poor by leaving a legacy – for those days a sizeable sum. The sum she left was to be invested. Half the annual interest was to be spent on the church fabric and half on the local poor. But, taking a rather dim view of the morals of the poor, she stipulated that they were not to receive their portion in cash, lest the gin palaces reaped the benefit. The church was to purchase bread and coal and dole them out at stated intervals. Should the church fail to perform this office, they would forfeit their share to some other charity.

The churchwardens of the time, whose job it has been to administer all this, have long regarded their duties as an anachronism and a flaming nuisance. None of the modern poor are being appreciably helped by the tiny quantities of bread and coal distributed and nobody has really wanted them for years.

Furthermore, the annual interest on the capital paid to the church was peanuts by modern standards.

Accordingly, we approached the Charity Commission with a view to winding up the whole business. Under modern law, I understand that this can be done. The outcome was a suggestion that the capital should be realised and divided in half. Half would be handed over to the civil authority to be used for some public amenity; and the other half would go to church funds.

This seemed to me to be a reasonable modern interpretation of her late Ladyship's wishes.

I was wrong, and the recent meeting has told me so – forcibly. I started by stating briefly the terms of the charity and the reasons behind the proposal to wind it up.

'Does that mean we've lost our rights?' asked Mr Demos truculently (as usual).

'It means,' I said, 'that there will be no further distribution of bread and coal, which has recently pretty well gone by default anyway'.

'Those rights,' said Mr Demos, 'are part of the parish. You have no business to take them away.'

Someone then pointed out that, by the terms of the trust, the church would not get any money if bread and coal were not provided. And this observation led to the totally illogical conclusion that the motive of the exercise was to cheat the poor of the parish in order to make more money for the church.

Thus two or three noisy elements, who never supported the church in any way at any time, were now insisting that the church was robbing the poor and that I was personally responsible.

Someone 'on my side' told me afterwards that word was going round that 'by law' if the charity was wound up, all the money had to be shared out between the holders of the rights.

Nothing will budge these opinions and any outsider would laugh them to scorn. Being involved I must learn to live with them.

The charity will be wound up and some, led by Mr Demos, will carry their grievance to the grave, or the crematorium, whichever is relevant.

9
The Vicar's Wife

1 March

I do not quite know what Christine would make of this chapter. I had better hide it in a drawer.

Vicar's Wife Syndrome may be summarised in the following way. If the vicar is a good pastoral priest doing his job, he may be at home only when he is getting under his wife's feet as she is trying to tidy his study. For the rest of the time, he is out in the parish attending functions or visiting the wolves. She may well find that she is providing a good home and well-prepared meals for a casual visitor while she is just part of the scenery.

Moreover, the vicar who is out among his flock for hours at a time will usually get on good terms with them – and very good terms with some of them. In spite of the Sunday press, there is normally nothing even vaguely immoral about these 'good terms' but, as one vicar's wife so clearly said, 'morality is not enough.'

A vicar's wife without a young family may feel neglected and lonely, while her outgoing husband – such a wonderful shepherd beloved of his sheep (and even of the wolves) – is quite unaware of it.

Vicars' wives face this threat in one of three ways:

1. They may take over, determined not to be unnoticed.
2. They may opt out and do their own thing.
3. They may work out what being a 'helpmeet' to their husband means and, with praiseworthy self-denial, get on with it.

The first type run the parish. Whether this is due to a love of bossiness or the conviction that their husbands are totally incompetent and must be protected from their own unworldliness I do not know. I do know that it can be overdone and the protected one may need protection from his over-managing spouse.

This type, if they really get into their stride, may accomplish much. They may order the set-up and decoration of the church, lay down forms of service and the nature of parish activities, pontificate on theology and doctrine, veto the decisions of the PCC and cause quite spectacular offence among important parishioners.

I have known a frustrated bishop, making a business call on a vicar to discuss church matters, finding himself interviewing the wife, while the helpless husband looks on. And he cannot get rid of the lady without being much ruder than his godly nature permits. Mrs Proudie is, of course, the archetype of this phenomenon.

The second group go to the other extreme. Their contribution to parish life is nil. They probably have a job, and live lives quite separate from the local public. Some of them seldom, if ever, go to church. These are probably the cheated ones, those who never married a clergyman in the first place but had to tag along as well as they might when their spouses heard, and answered, the call to the priesthood later in life. There is little harm in this, unless the parishioners insist on expecting a vicar's wife to do all sorts of things in the parish and cannot accept that they have, for all practical purposes, a bachelor vicar.

Or maybe the working wife thinks that her husband has nothing whatever to do all day, and can therefore take over all the household chores.

The third type is the true helpmeet. She makes a good home, feeds the brute, puts him right gently when he forgets to put his clerical collar on or fails to leave his muddy shoes outside the back door. She accepts cheerfully his untidiness, his absent-mindedness and general eccentricity, takes part in parish life without bossing it, visits people and is friendly to all.

Needless to say, Christine fall into this last category, otherwise

I would not have dared to write this chapter. It is part of her passport to Heaven, and when she gets there I hope the Lord will commend her generously for the wonderful person she has been.

I shall probably forget.

10
A Perfect Wife

8 March

An article on clergy wives, such as I had the courage (or foolhardiness) to pen last week, at once opens the door to the battle between modern feminists and Saint Paul. I wish we could arrange a meeting between the two. The flying fur would make good entertainment.

Paul, as I understand him, building on the Genesis story, maintains staunchly that woman is subservient to man and should regard him as her 'head'. Let the man rule and be master in his own house, while the woman is a helpmeet, who, presumably, smoothes his domestic path by getting on with the work.

The word 'inferior', if used, naturally gets women on the raw. But the ladies make false deductions if they think that 'inferiority' means, of necessity, that they are despised, crushed or humiliated. In fact, to counter any such notice, Paul insists that the husband must love his wife, thus putting paid to any suggestion of tyranny, oppression, male chauvinism or self-centred lack of appreciation.

In my less abstracted moments I can see that a woman's daily round in the home – cooking, washing and cleaning – can be tedious and uninspiring. But why should it be humiliating? If it all contributes to making a happy home, even the humblest of jobs has its point. George Herbert got the message when the mood of hymn-writing was upon him.

Some of the lady wolves in the parish seem to think that they can only find satisfaction in life if they are doing what is traditionally a man's job; and they will denounce Saint Paul accordingly. Incidentally, they are by no means the only group who will accept half a biblical passage, and fail to think through the remainder. We must understand, in this context, that Paul's vision was a happy home where man and wife have different but complementary functions.

Christine, I may say, plays her part in the Christian ménage nobly. She accepts, in practice as well as in theory, that service is more rewarding than status, and our family is greatly blessed accordingly. Saint Paul, she often says, was not completely bonkers.

Unfortunately, though, we are none of us perfect, and, when I am at my most critical (and self-righteous), I may wonder whether Christine and some other clergy wives have still some way to go to enter the top class.

I have in mind the writings of King Lemuel, which he managed to get published as an attachment to the Book of Proverbs. Following a moral lecture from his dragon of a mother on the virtues of the perfect king, he replies with a lecture on the perfect wife, whose price is 'above rubies'.

Her aim in life is to 'do her husband good'. Her programme in pursuit of this admirable goal is roughly as follows.

1. She gets up before dawn to prepare meals and order the servants about, for, even with her personal schedule, the servants still have something to do.

2. She goes to the market and shops around, for only the best is good enough for her family.

3. She buys wool and material and works willingly sewing and knitting – she makes all the family clothes and of the best quality materials. And, in her spare time, she will fill in with the manufacture of carpets and rugs.

4. She looks after the family business, managing the estate to its profit. The accounts are entirely her scene and she will sit up all night if necessary to balance the books and make them intelligible to the auditor.

5. Having thus dealt with her own home, she improves the family finances by making clothes to sell in the market.

6. Finally, she supports charities and entertains her

neighbours, whom she treats to profound and improving words of wisdom.

And what does her husband do while all this is going on? Respected and admired by all, he sits in his club (or, one supposes, in the saloon bar) with his cronies, putting the world to rights.

I wonder whether King Lemuel ever existed. If he did, I suspect, from the context, that he was giving his mother a tongue-in-cheek backhander she richly deserved.

But what a wonderful clergy wife this 'above rubies' treasure would make. And what a major disaster her husband would be as a parish priest.

11
The Food of Love

15 March

> If music be the food of love, play on. Give me excess of it [...][1]

So said Shakespeare. But notice the 'if'. I recollect Shelley's famous poem, as later edited by J B Morton. It is entitled 'To a lady singing':

> Music, when soft voices die,
> Vibrates in the memory.
> Heaven be praised, she's shut her row,
> But memory's an earthquake now.

It is to my shame that such thoughts should arise when I have been listening to, for example, the carols from King's College, Cambridge. If music is the food of love, when and under what circumstances does love rise to the bait?

Carols may bear a little analysis. To a great number of people, the singing or hearing of their favourite carols helps to inspire worship of the baby Jesus and feelings of goodwill to men. Carols may indeed feed love.

It is, therefore, with hesitation amounting to inhibition that I would like to confess to my parishioners that I am allergic to some carols – and on musical grounds.

Maybe my taste in music is not up to scratch, but, even if helped by modern harmonisation and arrangement, such efforts

---

[1] *Twelfth Night* I.i.1–3.

as 'The First Noel' fail to move me to any emotion approaching love.

As for the words of many of them… But, happily, we are only discussing music. Suffice it to say that some of the lyrics feed us with feelings quite averse to love.

To return to music. There is much modern music composed, according to the cynical, by persons devoid of musical inspiration, who are therefore obliged to concoct new forms or combinations of timbre and dynamic. The cognoscenti call the result 'sound'. The philistines call it 'noise'. Either may stimulate the intellect, but intellect is not love.

Then there is the whole 'pop' culture. The phenomenon of the Beatles, for example, fed something in human nature in a big way. But was it love? Being more or less tone-deaf to this sort of music myself, I am not in a position to say.

It is certain that primitive emotions are stimulated among the young by this culture. It has a fantastic appeal. But what do the big pop festivals actually do to the devotees? We may put aside, for the sake of argument, the unpleasant sidelines of these occasions, from the sanitary arrangements to the drug-pushing, and again concentrate on the music, which is often produced by highly gifted and competent performers. To the listeners does it do more than satisfy the urge for light entertainment?

Probably yes! In primitive societies, the rhythmic beat of the drums stirs the warriors to military action. To what extent modern rhythms and the accompanying dancing stir our youth to sexual activity I cannot say; probably a good deal less than elderly puritans like to imagine. I just do not know.

In so far as it does, it might be called the 'food of love'. But that requires a definition of love. What is called love in modern novels and newspapers and magazines may be given less flattering titles in circles with less permissive standards.

One of my favourite pieces of music is Brahms' *Requiem*. It gets me, and I am hooked! And, though the composer was an agnostic, he was a very sincere and thoughtful agnostic who has well caught the spirit of the biblical words he chose to set. Words and music are truly wed, and stir great emotions of sympathy and understanding.

These are ingredients of love; and, as I contemplate – *ouch!* – that band over the road has started, and will continue with its thump, thump, thump far into the night. Brahms is in full flight and thoughts of murder fill my mind.

Shakespeare's 'if' should really be written in capitals and underlined twice.

12
One of Us

22 March

There are many of us clergy who are 'good with young people', and I remember one fellow sheep who was so good with them that the young teenagers in his church even went as far as to call him 'one of us'.

He was interested in them, cared about them, used them in the church, and they responded. The generation gap almost disappeared. It seemed a great success story.

But beneath the surface, he was not so happy about it. He realised that, though he had all this youth support in the church, they were not being converted. If they could accept their vicar as 'one of us', they did not extend the privilege to the Lord he represented.

When their leader (for there was a leader among them) decided he was an atheist and broke away from the Church, most of the others went with him. They just lost interest.

No doubt good seed had been sown. But evangelism had not really scored high marks.

I think of the service at which I was instituted to the living of Chilford. The presiding bishop urged me to 'go out among my parishioners where they were' and mix with them – in the pub, in the marketplace and in any parish gathering that was in people's diaries. In other words I was being called to be 'one of us'.

I was not too enthusiastic about this, because I am a loner by nature and have never frequented public bars. I consulted Cedric on the subject.

All he would say was, 'Careful! Careful!'

Then I remembered a priest I once knew. He was as sociable as fleas on a dog – jolly, friendly and a frightfully good fellow. He was the life and soul of a party, and he went to them all. 'After all,' he would say, 'Jesus dined with the unrighteous and blessed the wine at a wedding, didn't he?'

Yet he felt increasingly dissatisfied with his life. He realised that Jesus did a lot of other things besides attending parties and blessing wine. He lived rough, identified with the outcast and distressed and brought healing to minds and bodies. He was, frankly, no socialite as my friend understood the term.

This priest repented, drastically cut down his social engagements and set about the task he was ordained to do in imitation of his Master. He said later that he now had fewer acquaintances, but many more friends.

Saint Paul, no mean Christian, said that he became 'all things to all men' that he might gain a few friends. This sounds so sensible, so right! But it is very difficult when we remember that it means we must be 'in the world, but not of it'.

Those who, like myself, feel so alienated in our faith from the general run of secular and not very godly men and women, may well be tempted to go along with the world, agree with the world's opinions, eat, drink and be merry with the world and be nice to such people as we have time for. But it may prove a very slippery slope. Having sacrificed dignity and respect, we may become so much 'one of us' with sinners that we become 'one of us' with sin.

Cedric will not have this. He will not have it at all.

If we get too familiar with youth, for example, we may well find that some of them merely despise us and let us down. Some probably will not. Either way, there is considerable substance in the remark of a committed Christian American teenager who said, 'We do want adults that really care about us, but we don't want them as pals.'

I have been too pally in my time. It has mixed benefits.

Jesus himself is the only safe guide. He mixed with sinners and helped them. He identified with those sick in mind or body and healed them. But he never accommodated the world's values and was extremely outspoken to those religious persons who did.

Apart from the Cross, he maintained his dignity because of what he is and has so gained the love and lasting devotion of millions.

Jesus came down to our level in order to bring us up to his. And we priests are meant to be his agents.

13
Mr Demos

29 March

Perhaps I ought to devote a chapter to my *bête noire* – the blackest of black wolves in my pack – Mr Demos.

The problem is that, at every Communion service, the Lord reminds me that I must love my neighbour as myself; and Mr Demos is undoubtedly my neighbour.

I dislike him quite a lot.

It is fashionable these days to argue that people who are a pain in the neck cannot help their condition. Their aggressive, disruptive or antisocial habits are either in their genes or are the results of a deprived childhood. What do I know of George Demos as a small boy? I presume he was one once.

He was of relatively humble birth, but certainly not deprived in any worldly sense. The Demos family lived in a semi-detached suburban residence with a garage outside and all the usual mod cons within.

His father was a butcher and his mother a conscientious but subservient housewife who did as she was told, or else!

George was the eldest of three children.

His two sisters were much of an age, but considerably younger than he was. Unkind persons whispered that the family increase was impeded for four or five years because the butcher went hunting with an alien pack until the Methodist church to which he belonged persuaded him that conjugal fidelity counted for something. Lower middle-class respectability became the order of the day.

Cedric keeps telling me that I should eschew my delight in

such titbits of gossip, so let me try to explain Mr Demos without these side issues. I will attempt to proceed charitably.

The boy Demos was bright and went to grammar school, where he made his mark as an efficient leader of other boys.

His father was proud of him and repeatedly told him so. Between them, they decided that university would be a waste of time and opportunity, and that his talents were sufficiently developed for him to rise swiftly in some practical commercial undertaking. He was apprenticed to a firm of surveyors and made good.

And then his powers of leadership went to his head. From being a young man in Chilford, he took part in every local activity, from local government to the management of the village hall. And everything he touched, he ran.

Being a lifelong churchman, and having gravitated to Anglicanism from his father's adherence to the Methodist persuasion, he also touched the parish church, and so had to run that as well.

When I was appointed vicar of Chilford, he had been church-warden for a number of years. And did we know it! He runs the church as he runs the village. 'Thus says Mr Demos…'

To be more honest than I want to be, there is much to be said for him as a churchwarden. He understands finance, is a capable administrator and a conscientious worker. And he lives a life of moral rectitude that the tongue of scandal has (so far) been unable to tarnish.

At first, as expected, all was well. He gave me a good welcome, showed me the ropes and was most anxious that Christine and I were comfortable in the vicarage. But in those days he was the master, telling the new boy how to find his way about. The wolf was not yet ready to devour the lamb. Let him get a little older and fatter.

The first inkling I had of trouble was on the occasion when he started telling me who I ought to visit in the parish and who I ought not. The 'oughts' were the nice people of good social standing.

Then, as I found my feet, I developed ideas of my own. Most of these found little favour with Mr Demos who was, on the surface, one of the 'as-it-was-in-the-beginning-it-now-and-ever-shall-be' brigade.

'In the beginning' refers to the time when Mr Demos really got started ordering everyone else about. From that point, we graduated to the stage when anything I said had to be contradicted and everything I did adversely criticised, not necessarily because Mr Demos disagreed with them but because I was saying or doing them. 'Getting one's knife into someone' explains the principle involved.

Mr Demos and I are enemies and Jesus says we must love our enemies. I wonder how Jesus would deal with Mr Demos.

I try to envisage the man in the role of Nicodemus, the church leader who wanted to serve God and the Truth and came to Jesus for advice. But I cannot get Caiaphas out of my head.[1]

---

[1] Caiaphas was the Jewish high priest who organised the plot to kill Jesus.

14

By Their Fruits…

5 April

How gratifying it is when we vicars stand at the church door at the end of a service, shaking hands with the departing sheep and receiving their plaudits: 'Lovely service, Vicar,' 'Excellent sermon – just what I've always said myself,' and so on. It all gives one that nice warm feeling inside normally associated with a pat on the back.

Occasionally, though, I sense a little devil in the porch roof sniggering at all this euphoria. 'And what,' I ask, 'are you finding so funny?'

He does not tell me, of course. With Cedric's help I have to work it out.

I had an inkling a month or so ago. One of our deanery clergy was required to preach at some special service. With all the praise accorded to my own sermons from time to time, I had reason to think that I was the man for the job. I presumed that I would be asked.

I was not asked. The job was offered to, and accepted by, the Reverend Basil Peabody, of all men; a young man I despise as a 'modernist' and clerical whiz-kid.

I was hurt and predicted failure for the service. I would have preached the simple gospel, clear and unadulterated. God knows what liberal heresies we were destined to hear flowing from the mouth of this inexperienced amateur Don Cupitt, who evidently thought of himself as some sort of revolutionary Elijah.

I was faced with the unpalatable truth that, even if local congregations did shower my words with praise – and perfectly sincere praise at that – my fellow clergy and other Church leaders did not necessarily think I was the bee's pyjamas or whatever, and would just as soon listen to someone else.

When I had calmed down a bit, Cedric had his word.

'This latest outburst of yours – a touch of jealousy, perhaps? Or merely a case of sour grapes?'

I am put in mind of the case of David Watson, that remarkable young evangelist who led an extraordinary church revival in York during the 1970s. Great numbers of all ages found a new love for their Lord and church services had to be relayed into the hall and duplicated until a much larger church was provided in the city centre.

At a large conference of all the diocesan clergy, he was asked to explain his phenomenal success and a meeting was called. It was attended by a fair number of clergy of all shapes, sizes and ages, those who had, in their various ways, laboured in the Lord's sheepfold with far less success than had David.

When he had had his say, and said it with remarkable humility, an elderly vicar rose to his feet. He was quivering with passion. He wished to know why this young man, little more than half his own age, had had the gall – almost the impertinence – to call a meeting to tell us older and more experienced clergy how to do the job. He was very angry.

I recollect that David remained quite calm. He simply said that he had been asked to speak of his experiences, and all he had done was to seek the guidance of the Holy Spirit, and had been led by that Spirit accordingly.

Some of us cannot bear to think that others may be making a greater success of their ministries than we are, especially if the other is younger and more energetic.

It is certainly encouraging to be told that one's efforts are helpful or inspiring to others. But, even at my most exalted, I must remember that I am not Mr Big. At best, I can but be a human channel for the love of Him who humbled himself to the ignominy of a criminal's death, and so became the Biggest of them all. And it does not matter who else he is choosing.

'And don't you forget it,' said Cedric to me last night.

'And don't you keep rubbing it in,' I snarled back.

15
Inflation

12 April

We are going through one of those periodic national panics about money. The official patter is all too familiar: 'We are living beyond our means. We must cut down on government expenditure. No wage claims to be in excess of the rate of inflation,' and so on.

Normally these pious statements are followed by politicians awarding themselves salary increases far in excess of those they are trying to impose on others. And, if the increase is sufficiently large to bring the blush of shame to ministerial cheeks, much of it can, of course, be called 'expenses of office'.

At the same time, firms in financial difficulties may 'rationalise' their businesses by freezing or beating down their employees' pay claims or cutting staff while voting to grant already vastly overpaid directors simply enormous increases in fees.

If challenged, those who hold the purse strings may always find good excuses for what they do. Even so, it seems to the simple-minded, such as myself, that economy is regarded as something that must be practised by other people, and that, if charity begins at home, sacrifice certainly does not. I find it all very puzzling. With more interest in morality than high finance, it just does not add up for me.

The puzzle is not entirely confined to the secular world. The Anglican Church, for example, is usually in a tizzy about money. 'How are we going to make ends meet?' and so forth.

One day, I arose at a diocesan synod to shoot my great mouth off concerning five items in the diocesan budget. Redundant churches and the emoluments of the stewardship adviser were two of them. I was not criticising. I simply wanted to know what the sums allocated to these five objects were actually spent on.

I received five answers, not one of them an answer to the questions I had asked. I received the impression – probably quite unfairly – that it was not quite in good taste to raise such issues. Our financial officials are honest men and we may assume that they will spend our money in the best way possible.

And then an elderly cleric rose and caught the eye of the chairman. He suggested that, at a time when the nation's workers were being called to tighten their belts, it might be a good thing if we clergy accepted a reduction in our stipends by way of example.

For one terrible moment I feared that the bishop would rise and rend his garments. But happily the suggestion was accepted as merely heretical rather than blasphemous. Following an embarrassed silence, the finance man explained, as to a child, that such a move was impossible. It might upset the books or muddle the accounts or something like that. I really cannot remember exactly.

Yet again, as I sit writing, I remember another conference about falling income. The half-crown had become obsolete. Thus, it was argued, those who contributed a half-crown to the church collection would only now relieve themselves of a florin, as being the largest coin in circulation.

A wise man rose and spoke.

'We want more money and we do not know where it is coming from,' he said. 'I'll tell you. It is coming from our pockets. If prices are rising, so are most of our incomes.'

Perhaps the faithful added to their covenants and envelope schemes or put two florins in the bag. I do not know. I do know that there was no extra crisis when the half-crown passed away.

The problem keeps raising its ugly head and the wail about approaching disaster through rising prices has been with us as long as I can remember. Individuals suffer, no doubt, but anything like national disaster is constantly postponed.

Maybe the doom watch people have left something out of their calculations. Or maybe the Lord, as we flounder about in the toils of Mammon (and greed) is quietly putting his oar in and leading the faithful through the financial wilderness in his own way.

Finance is beyond me. I had better turn my attention to the Kingdom of God and leave the workings of Mammon to the experts.

16
Public Meeting

19 April

I have been among the wolves and right into the heart of their territory. For nowhere are wolves more at home than at a public meeting called to discuss some public project.

In Chilford, Mr Demos is always present, a guarantee that any sheep of a peaceful or conciliatory disposition will be fallen upon, torn to pieces and devoured. For Mr Demos must be master of all he surveys and has no patience with any who dare to question that position.

Sometimes the matter under discussion for the parish council is a minor one – the extension of someone's house or the diversion of a footpath. But today's issue was a much larger affair.

Spies from the Board of Trade believe that there are deposits of oil beneath Chilford and they intend to have them investigated.

The meeting was called to open the matter up to the residents.

Small or great, it was certain that war would break out. There was bound to be violent opposition to any change in the village status quo; though the Demos voice, which is the loudest and most aggressive, works with a Demos-inclined slant.

Anything proposed by Mr Demos must be pushed through vigorously, scattering rules and regulations to the winds. Anything proposed by anyone else must be resisted with all the force his self-importance can command.

The proceedings started in hostile silence. A gentleman from the Ministry, naturally pre-oiled, explained carefully the benefits to the community that would come should oil prove commercial. More people would come into the village. Local tradesmen would be helped and employment found for local people. Modern technology would keep despoliation of the countryside to a minimum, the necessary earthworks would be hidden largely by trees and rehabilitation of the landscape would be carried out directly while the drills were working.

The speaker produced a large-scale map of the area marked with the spots where they proposed to put the drilling rigs and necessary offices. The audience was invited to come up and examine the map, if they wished.

Mr Demos, who considered that he was the audience, came up and gave the map a cursory glance, after which he returned to his place without comment. I, who know the signs, was aware that he was mustering his gifts of overbearing rudeness to do battle.

Hostility increased as questions of details ensued, some of which proved very difficult to answer. These questions varied from the sensible ('How long is the setting up of this scheme likely to take?') to the ridiculous. Mr Demos rose to add to the latter.

'It does not seem to have occurred to you,' he said, 'that your office will be built bang in the line of the view of Bilchester Cathedral from my windows.'

The man from the Ministry remained calm, but had to confess that the Board of Trade had not really spent a great deal of time considering the view from the Demos windows.

I happen to know that Mr Demos' statement was, as a matter of fact, quite untrue. But Mr Demos is anti-oil and so his guns must be loaded with any sort of ammunition, however frivolous. And this particular shell, when it exploded, did have the desired effect of transferring the whole argument from the realms of public utility and welfare to that of environment.

Tempers rose.

I was surprised to see how many pro-oils there were present. But, as usual, neither the pros nor the antis were capable of discussing the issue calmly on its merits. The arguments, such as they were, became steadily more personal and abusive.

I have sometimes observed that, when politicians have nothing sensible to say, they spray their opponents with nauseating moral opprobrium and character assassination. Our meeting swiftly sank to that level. Pros and antis accused each other of being liars, cheats and ignorant nobodies who did not know what they were talking about.

Eventually order was more or less restored and Mr Demos, ignoring the chairman, delivered his *'coup de disgrace'*.

'This meeting,' he said, 'is an utter waste of time! You people in your London offices have no interest in our ways. You concoct these schemes entirely for your own benefit and they are all cut-and-dried before you come here. On behalf of everyone in this village, I tell you, sir, that your project will be fought tooth and nail at every step.'

I make no comment. My scene is Christian behaviour and cooperation and I spent that evening in a totally foreign country.

17

Wolves at the Door

26 April

The vicarage doorbell, like the telephone, may be an inconvenience, especially if one is too tired (or too lazy) to answer it. Firmly settled in your favourite armchair before the fire, with light entertainment on the goggle-box, one is apt to forget that peoples' troubles do not always coincide with gaps in your favourite programmes.

To a certain extent one may plead deafness: 'I'm so sorry, I never heard the bell.' Then the onus of answering the door and dealing with whatever lurks outside falls on the wife, who, happily, is a splendid Christian woman, patient, long-suffering and far better at dealing sympathetically with wolves than is he whose half-consciousness is centred on *Tom and Jerry*.

If not a parishioner or personal friend, the visitor is likely to be someone selling junk or hard-luck stories. Purveyors of insurance or those offering fantastic lottery prizes in exchange for negligible outlay will use the post or the telephone.

Cedric tells me to grieve for the junk merchants. They are often out-of-work youths with little substance between the ears who are exploited by those who prey upon the unfortunate for personal gain. Some are really nice kids, well worth the gift of a cup of tea, a slice of the wife's cake, a brief experience of the study fire and the passage of a pound or two in exchange for a short chat and a small pile of threadbare dishcloths.

The hard-luck wolves are cast in a different mould. They are mostly scavenger types. Their heart-rending tales may be ignored. They are on the road because they prefer it that way and, for one reason or another, will have nothing to do with rules and regulations. This does not mean that one does not wish to help them to a better way of life, but there it is.

Clergy are soft touches because we are (maybe) so compassionate. If not that, we are richer than they are, and Saint Paul tells us somewhere not to bother if we are cheated a bit.

So let's treat them to a bite or two, or a little gift they may squander as they will. We cannot really 'help' them without befriending them and engaging them in protracted heart-to-hearts, and there are practical difficulties in the way of that.

But who are those 'ravening wolves, seeking whom they may devour' of whom Jesus warns us in Matthew 7:15? That peal on the bell may herald the arrival of the Devil, but it is more likely to indicate the attentions of Jehovah's Witnesses, who will nowadays talk to the clergy sometimes.

These good people have had a certain success with some of my congregation and this annoys me. I tell myself that I preach the true gospel and the Witnesses butt in and steal my sheep.

Yet there are many homes where they inspire something akin to terror. Doors are hastily shut upon them and well-bred persons can scarcely bring themselves to be civil.

When Cedric is not listening, I tend to find this gratifying. They are open enemies of the established churches which (or so they insist) preach 'false religion', and it pleases me when they meet slammed doors.

In this mood of self-satisfaction, I recently called on some newcomers on our council estate, not a very godly area. The door was opened by a man in his shirtsleeves. He fled to the back regions without a word to be replaced by a woman who was polite but very much on the defensive.

I had called as a gentle sheep, only desiring to be friendly. I was received, instinctively, as a slavering wolf waiting to leap upon the prey within to tear it to pieces. I was, in fact, receiving the Jehovah's Witness treatment I had rejoiced to see inflicted on others.

It all happened to the King of Love himself, when he sought the lost sheep. Those who wished to be found received him gladly. Those who did not ran from him in terror. They still do.

18
Retreat

3 May

I am in retreat. It is bliss.

Clergy are urged to take one day off a week. That is splendid.

Their churchwardens are told to insist that they have a proper annual holiday away from it all. This is better, even when divorced from that old chestnut about the incumbent who reported that there was never anything improper about his holidays anyway.

But retreats are best of all, because you have the moral satisfaction of knowing that you are, in theory, recharging your spiritual batteries, a sheep to be shorn of its worries, the better to face afresh the rough and tumble of life among the wolves.

Our diocesan retreat house is situated in glorious country. And, although some retreat conductors cannot stop talking, ours, happily, is a devotee of beautiful silence. We are encouraged to benefit accordingly.

The weather is perfect and I spend the afternoons sitting in a deckchair on the terrace, admiring the view and thinking beautiful thoughts.

I think of the things from which I am escaping. Church income was down last year and expenses are up this year. The architect has been on his routine inspection and warned of weather damage to the church fabric. If we do not have new locks on the cupboards and a lot more things kept in them, the insurance people will get nasty.

And, in the background, lurks the spectre of Mr Demos, arguing with everything I say, constantly telling me what I ought to do and finding fault when I do it. How that man dislikes me! And how mutual are my feelings!

A savage nudge from Cedric reminds me that these are not beautiful thoughts. I am here to meditate on God and the things of God. I should be thinking positively.

Very well. I will think about God. He is God of all the earth. He is not only the God of the Christians, but also of the Muslims, the Hindus, the Buddhists and all. A comforting thought. In spite of so many sectarian differences, we are all going the same way, though by different routes. Or so some starry-eyed persons tell me.

I cannot altogether agree. There are notably all those cults who brainwash young people, have their own moral standards and may even end in mass suicide on the grounds that the world is so irredeemably evil that the only thing to do is to clear out of it.

I can admire the moral standards and the discipline of the Muslim but his methods of maintaining them can be too violent for my liking.

There are variants of Hinduism that are most attractive. To follow a guru, do yoga exercises to harmonise body, mind and spirit or practise transcendental meditation and spend your time in an aura of peace, freedom and love has its good points – lots of them – especially if you are unaware that so many cult leaders are bogus psychopaths.

I think I might be a Buddhist monk, eschewing all desire and seeking nirvana, when the soul loses itself in the universal Soul. What bliss!

I drift off to sleep in the sunshine, dream about wolves, and wake to find Cedric waiting to lecture me.

'You idle clod!' he says. 'If you think you are on this earth just to save your own miserable little soul, you are merely revealing what a miserable little soul it is. Does nobody else matter to you?

'What about all those parishioners who love you and support you? What about those who are uplifted by your sermons, helped by your counsels and stimulated by your friendship? What about Christine – a wife in a thousand – who shares your ideals and does so much to help you achieve them? And what about all those in your spiritual charge who do not know God and are unaware that Jesus loves them?

'It seems that all these you are ready to ignore so that you may rest in airy-fairy peace. Stir yourself and face up to the challenges of church finance, fabric, insurance and Big Bad Wolf Demos who is waiting to devour you.

'Don't let him. You know that God is with you. Make sure that you are with him.'

Quite!

19

Bait for the Wolves

10 May

I have heard it all before, and no doubt I shall hear it all again, many times over. 'The Church must change radically, bring itself up to date, adapt itself to modern thinking, appeal to the masses,' and so on.

This time it is the Reverend Basil Peabody, the present incumbent of Claybourne. He is a youngish man, full of zeal for reform. Liberal in his theology, he accepts any fresh idea he reads about as progressive wisdom.

He wishes to rebuild Claybourne church as a social centre rather than what he calls a 'shrine of merely historical interest', and he is all for 'meeting people where they are' without considering that they might be better off somewhere else.

At our last chapter meeting, he took the floor and expounded his theories at tedious length. He told us what most of us have been aware of for a very long time – that the Church is totally out of touch with the majority of our people. He maintains that only a completely new start – under his leadership – can put things right.

I might have listened with more sympathy and understanding to his sweeping generalisations had they been delivered with just a *soupçon* of humility. But I am some twenty years older than the Reverend Basil Peabody and my hackles rise when I am treated as a traditionalist has-been of no significance whatsoever.

When I got the chance to speak, my voice was pregnant with sarcasm and entirely devoid of the milk of human kindness.

'And how,' I asked, 'do you propose to implement this noble revolution?'

The floodgates of his oratory were reopened, and a fresh rush of verbiage released. He reminded me of politicians in opposition fighting an election without any positive programme to put forward. They spend most of their time denouncing the record, the ineptitude, the faithlessness and the criminal dishonesty of the existing rulers, filling in with high-sounding clichés about 'building a new Britain' and so on, hopefully promoting in their listeners ideas of hope, purpose and prosperity.

Applied to the Church, this means a dreary recital of past and present failure to communicate, adverse criticism of bishops, scorn for the ineffectiveness of other clergy and the uselessness of standard church services.

Applied to me personally, it means the outpourings of an insolent and ignorant young puppy. I resent it.

I resent the assumption that any theological opinion, thought to be new, is therefore progressive and supersedes any other traditional belief, especially when I recognise many of these 'modern' ideas as ancient heresies dressed up in modern clothes, most of them known to and refuted by Saint Paul.

I resent this young man lecturing us – we who have been thinking things over much longer than he has and can therefore see much more clearly the snags in his revolutionary ideas.

In fact, I resent so much about that young Peabody that I am liable to forget Matthew 5:22: 'Whosoever shall say (to his brother), "thou fool" shall be in danger of the hell of fire.' May not this young man's opinions be as good as mine?

Cedric butts in.

'Because Christian truth is not a matter of personal opinion. It is not even a matter of majority opinion. Christian theology is God's opinion as it is expressed in the teachings of Christ recorded in the Gospels. It has to be interpreted and understood, not contradicted or improved upon.'

Well! That's custard pie treatment for some clerical faces. And that certainly goes for the Irreverent Basil Peabody.

But, am I not being a little harsh? He may mellow in time and some of his ideas may prove to be God's truth. What does the Bible say?

The Bible says that God resists the proud and it is the cardinal sin of pride that is really the point at issue here.

If I resist this young upstart, then I am on the Lord's side.

Cedric again.

'Tell me, are you so het up about Basil because he thinks he knows better than God, or because he has insulted you personally?'

I sometimes wish that Cedric would keep his trap shut.

20
Black Dog

17 May

I am depressed. There seems to be no real purpose in life. Nothing appears worth doing and I have no desire to do it anyway. In the words of Shakespeare's Hamlet, 'all is stale, flat and unprofitable.'

Normally I am conscientious about my duties but I did not go to church this morning to recite the daily office. What's the use? Nobody ever joins me, and I can read the lessons and psalms just as well at home, provided that I stir myself and get down to it.

I did get through the family Eucharist last Sunday, but it was not very inspiring. I read through the service, barely paying attention to the well-known words and with the sole object of reaching the end as speedily as possible. Happily, I had the sermon prepared and written out but it meant little to me and was delivered with the minimum of conviction. It must have been very boring.

Today is my official day off. We usually go out somewhere or I catch up with a bit of light reading, or tie up loose ends of easy business. Instead I am just sitting, aware that there is much that might – even ought to – be done.

It can wait until I feel like dealing with it. At present nothing interests me.

I don't know what the matter is. I am perfectly well physically and have no worries about my health. I feel vaguely sorry for Christine, who sees I am not myself and is clearly worried. But when she asks, I just say that I am OK because I am tongue-tied when I try to collect my thoughts into intelligible order.

Perhaps I am mentally ill. If so, I am not owning up. Maybe a psychiatrist could find out what is wrong, but I am having none of that! I have always hated the thought of discussing my deepest and most secret self with others. And even if I thought it was a good thing, I cannot bring myself to make an appointment with a head-shrinker.

Yet psychiatrists do get to the cause of things and, if I can find out what is really getting me down, I might feel better.

It may be the perpetual strain of feeling that I am not getting anywhere spreading the Christian faith. I know I normally take services well, but it seems to make no impact. And, although I know perfectly well that I can never know exactly what help I may be doling out unawares, it does appear that people are not responsive.

Mr Demos may well be having a disproportionate effect on me. It is all very well to make up my mind that I am going to ignore him, but he has a very wearing effect. All the time he hovers!

In my time, I have been bold enough to preach that illness – and in particular mental illness – may be the result of sinful thinking or behaviour. Applied to myself, I cannot work it out.

In my time, I have taught that, if things go wrong, God may be teaching us something. I pray, but God is silent.

I have consulted Cedric and we are evidently not on speaking terms.

I am not overworked and I do not want a holiday. I just want to sit and do nothing.

Yet, even if I try, I cannot lose my Christian faith, my certainty that God holds the reins and will see us through. 'The Lord chastens those he loves' and 'God will prune a fruitful tree to make it bear more fruit' are the gist of two encouraging thoughts.

★

Cedric has uttered at last. He reminds me that I am apt to be impatient with those suffering from self-pity and the 'black dog' syndrome. They should pull themselves together and get busy!

Perhaps a dose of it myself may teach me to be more sympathetic.

21

Lèse-majesté

24 May

'Bugger Vicar!'

Believe it or not, these words were recently uttered by a young boy as he passed me in the street.

I know the brat. Of course I do. He is one of my parishioners. He lives on the new estate. And the fact that his parents are not exactly a refined couple and their domestic arrangements and lifestyle hardly inspiring, in no way excuses the little horror.

What should I do?

I might have turned and given the child a sound ticking off. But I was taken off guard, and he is a good runner who would not have stayed within earshot a moment longer than necessary.

If I had been quick enough, I might have got in with a worthy clout over his obnoxious little face and so promoted a scandal that would have delighted the local press.

I might complain to the brat's parents. Father, should he be at home, would grunt and say nothing. Mother would tell me two flat lies:

1. that he never uses such language at home, and

2. that she would tell him about it.

I could go to the local schoolmaster, who would not want to be involved. He would tell me that the loathsome little beast is only six, comes from a rough home and one must make allowances.

In the event, I walked on, pretending that I had not heard. But my feelings are hurt. A vicar is, by virtue of his office, on a pedestal, and a dignified one at that. He should be treated with respect, even deference. These cases of *lèse-majesté* are just not on and something unpleasant – even drastic – should be visited on that child.

Come to think of it, we clergy are often treated contemptuously, even if the contempt is not so crudely expressed. In my time I have been told by teenagers that Christianity is 'just my opinion' and of no value compared with their atheistic ones. I have been sharply rebuked by the scoutmaster for suggesting that the church-sponsored scouts should be taken to church. I have had remarks from my sermons misquoted and misinterpreted to my detriment and the fact that certain bishops are in the same boat is small consolation. I have been accused (normally behind my back) of dishonesty and hypocrisy.

Mr Demos in particular has publicly thwarted and contradicted me as though I were an ignorant savage in church affairs. And Miss Rufflet once stormed at me because she had averred that I had said something to her out of deliberate malice 'because I hated her'.

These things can be very galling. I do love my parishioners – well, some of them. And I know I should love them all, even if I have not yet got round to Mr Demos. To be treated to this sort of unbalanced paranoia from neurotic people is not what I deserve.

Sometimes I get really depressed and I once asked Cedric how I ought to deal with these incidents. People should not be allowed to get away with these insults.

And Cedric said nothing. Absolutely nothing.

Christine did say something.

'Don't get so het up,' she said. 'Think of all those in the parish who support you, learn from you, are helped by you and, yes, love you: confirmation candidates who get the message, those uplifted by your sermons, those who really appreciate your visits and are genuinely concerned for God's work in the parish.'

A great woman, Christine. But even she got fed up with my moaning about the 'bugger, Vicar' incident.

'Who are you meant to be following?' she snapped.

'Jesus Christ, I suppose,' I said, lamely.

'Then follow him,' she said. 'And give us a break. You have

not been hit over the mouth, knocked about, spat on, nor crowned with thorns. Nor are you going to be crucified, with all your friends deserting you. And you deserve it much more than he did.

'And I might remind you of Saint Peter. When he suffered for Christ's sake, as perhaps you are in a very small way, he had the grace to be thankful.'

22
Sheep, Wolves or Goats?

31 May

I have recently attended a clergy chapter meeting and am engaged in a little introspection and soul-searching on behalf of that august body.

The Anglican priesthood throws up a number of strange characters. In theory, we are a group of Christians called by God to spread his gospel and help forward his work in the world. Our meetings should be cooperative assemblies considering how we may best serve the Lord in this great task.

It is possible for a chapter meeting to deteriorate into a group of very fallible mortals putting forth their individual views on social and theological questions, and merely deciding on those matters on which they agree to differ.

Perhaps an airing of everyone's opinions is intended to produce a balanced judgement on things. Frequently, it does no such thing. We seldom take much notice of what others say, unless we violently disagree with them. And there is nothing balanced about the Reverend Basil Peabody, the arrogant young so-and-so.

We have long since enjoyed the usual bickering about the Virgin Birth and the factual account of the Resurrection followed by the more vicious emotional brawl on such subjects as the ordination of women to the priesthood and gay clergy of all sexes.

The battleground is normally 'modern social conditions' and the opposing armies, broadly speaking, those steeped in existing order and the 'liberal' revolutionaries, 'Trads' versus 'Mods'.

After young Basil's latest outburst – on the subject of

comparative religion – I asked him outright, 'Are we meant to be serving God, or is he meant to be serving us?'

He gave me a fleeting, but nonetheless withering, look.

'God,' he said, 'is serving man. Jesus made that quite clear when he washed the disciples' feet.'

It seems to me that herein lies the real split in the Anglican Church, a far more serious split than most of the things we argue about. Is modern man supreme, free to decide his own fate with the promise that God will back him up and make the rough places smooth? Or are we called to help God in his work of reconciliation and salvation?

Put another way, do we love the Lord our God enough to want to serve him on his terms or do we patronise him enough to assume that he will add his blessing to anything we may think up in the pursuit of 'progress'?

Put even more concisely, who is the boss? God or modern man?

Basil Peabody has made it quite clear which side he is on.

'We must change our faith,' he says. 'Wipe the slate clean and start afresh.' And he has the arrogance to insist that, 'most people agree with me, but have not the courage to say so.'

I wish to make it quite clear that I oppose him totally.

It might be a good thing if the Lord made it quite clear to all of us that a house divided against itself shall not stand. If we Christians in a church cannot agree on the basics of our faith, we are heading for disaster.

It might be salutary for us to consider our Lord's one way of dealing with theological controversy.

He did not summon synods to discuss his teaching, nor did he ask everyone's opinion on the moral principles he laid down, deciding the issue by majority vote.

He said he spoke with the voice of God, without suggesting to his disciples that the truth of what he said depended on their approval or rejection of it.

In effect, he said: 'These are my words. You must understand them in the context of my command to love God and your neighbour as yourself but you are not at liberty to alter them to suit your own preferences or social theories.'

That's all right, then. I am on the Lord's side, one of the sheep, in fact. I pat myself on the back accordingly.

As for the Reverend Basil, perhaps I had better leave him to the Lord who has announced his intention of separating the sheep from the goats in his own way and in his own time.

23
Holiday

5 July

As a young sheep, how easy it was to experience a call to the priesthood, and to reckon thereby that one's faith would guarantee a life of calm self-assurance in which one fed hungry lambs with spiritual food and shed abroad one's love for all persons in a responsive and grateful parish.

Accordingly, when we are thrown to the wolves, there is usually a period when everything in the garden is lovely and the wolves are all dressed in sheep's clothing. We call it the 'honeymoon period'.

When we are aware of this fancy dress on the part of the wolves, the pressures start mounting. Administrative difficulties, problems of church maintenance and finance, showers of bumph from the diocesan office and specialist ministries, and the pinpricks – sometimes applied with the point of a dagger – from bossy, misguided or neurotic persons, all add considerable stress to the task of caring for the sick and needy and dispensing love wholesale.

How thoughtful of the powers that be to insist that we take a 'proper' holiday every year!

In my case, Mr Demos alone adds quite fifty per cent to the normal stresses of ministry and so it is perhaps not surprising that this year things have been getting me down and a break – real and far away – was very welcome.

My aged father, a generous man, offered Christine and myself the wherewithal to hire a holiday cottage, specifying only that it was right away from Chilford. We went to the Scilly Isles, leaving no address for forwarding mail. The cottage was not on the telephone, though we promised to ring our boy at boarding school once or twice.

The prospect was unalloyed paradise.

Of course, there were last minute difficulties. There always are. In this case, there were three. My head server – a youth of seventeen in whom I had great hopes as a pillar of the Church – rebelled against me and the Christian faith and went off to join a commune of some sort. Old Mrs Dunstable, one of the most faithful of the faithful, was removed, terminally ill, to hospital, and I did want to be present for her final pilgrimage. And the Church insurance people insisted on the immediate application of better locks and security measures in the church.

I did think that Mr Demos would cope with that last one. But, with what is now traditional cussedness on his part, he told me that he was not going to do my job for me. It could wait until I got back. And if the church was burgled meanwhile, it would be my responsibility.

Unhappily, we may 'get away from it all' but we have to take ourselves with us. And I am a worrier.

I know I should not be. Good Christians do not worry. They know, in practice as well as in theory, that the Lord is with them and will see them through as long as they trust him and cooperate. As Cedric keeps telling me, I am just not good enough.

But I do care about my parishioners and so I worry. I must have treated that boy wrongly and throughout my holiday I was going over and over in my mind the things I could possibly have done to encourage his defection. I could not rid myself of wondering daily about Mrs Dunstable. And I was in constant fear that the church would indeed be robbed in my absence and that the insurance people would refuse to pay up.

And what can I do, I asked myself daily, to control the Demos menace?

I worried about Chilford constantly.

I have returned home to find the servers' rota carrying on very well with one short. Mrs Dunstable is still alive ('Your prayers have helped me enormously, Vicar,') and my other churchwarden, with the active support of young Mr James, has had all the security work laid on, ignoring Mr Demos in the process.

But this has led to a new worry I had not anticipated. On the second Sunday of my absence, Mr Demos attended church as usual only to discover that the other two had dealt with the security. That was now his job and how dare they interfere?

There was a monumental row in the church porch after the service, a row that is still the talk of the parish and one that has upset the congregation in a very big way.

More than one has told me that I alone now keep them faithful, so unpleasant is the present atmosphere.

Why must Mr Demos cause all this unpleasantness?

24
A Break with Tradition

12 July

I have been, purely as an observer, to a meeting to discuss the future of the parish of Claybourne. The proposal is that it should be combined with Cherrybourne, of which I was vicar before I moved to Chilford.

The meeting was held in Claybourne church hall and was, in my cynical opinion, simply a piece of window dressing. The diocesan authorities have long since decided what they are going to do with Claybourne but they have to hold these meetings with the people concerned in order to show the green light to the spirit of democracy.

Let all have their say, and then let all be ignored.

In fact, the meeting showed the red light to local tradition and the wolves of Claybourne were out in force, ready to leap upon the ecclesiastical sheep who were daring to upset the status quo.

Claybourne is a village off the beaten track, a good deal smaller than neighbouring Cherrybourne, who, it is proposed, should absorb them. But Claybourne are fiercely independent and conscious of their own identity, which has to be maintained at all costs.

Consequently, all swords are unsheathed before the meeting begins. Unhappily, there is little solid ground for their objections to the merger, which only makes them more determined that it shall not take place.

The recently retired vicar had been there a very long time. By nature he was a recluse, and a lazy one at that. Church services had been conducted simply as a matter of rote, events that had to be got through at stated intervals. There were no church organisations and, though the people knew they had a vicar, they took practically no notice of him.

The church was badly attended, in poor repair and short of money. It had fallen very short in its dues to the diocese for several years.

Battle was joined by the archdeacon, leading the attack on behalf of the sheep in the upper echelons of the hierarchy and the diocesan board of finance. He explained that there was a shortage of clergy and that, even if a vicar could be provided for every parish, there would not be enough money to pay them anything like enough to make up the stipend expected nowadays. Financial reserves were used up, administrative expenses were rising all the time and congregations were being asked for more money than many of them could give.

The only answer was to amalgamate parishes and make one priest responsible for a much larger area. Smaller and poorer churches could then be helped by the larger and richer. Even so, if the church was to remain in existence, it would mean that a good deal of the vicar's traditional work must be done by the laity.

Claybourne's wolves counter-attacked with spirit and venom but they had no effective weapons. One said that they had always had a resident vicar and so it was their right to have one still. He liked to think that the church was there if he wanted it (which he didn't).

Another said that they had a good modern vicarage, which must, obviously, be inhabited by a vicar. It would be sacrilege to sell it.

One said that he did not often go to church (he meant never) but he did like to see a vicar walking about the place.

One prophesied that, should there be no resident vicar, the few that still went to church would immediately cease the practice.

And one particularly savage wolf told the archdeacon to his face that it was his duty to provide them with a vicar. He demanded that a list of available clergy be sent to them so that they might choose which one they would accept.

The archdeacon, an elderly man, was quite accustomed to this sort of ignorant challenge and merely asked how many ordinands Claybourne had provided within living memory. Why should they enjoy preferential treatment?

I found the whole procedure an interesting study. It was a straight fight between prejudiced local tradition and business expertise, with most of the cards in the hands of the latter.

There was no place on the agenda for the guidance of the Holy Spirit. I am of the school of thought that, if Christians are in difficulties, God is trying to teach them something. If the Anglican Church cannot afford to do God's work properly, what are we meant to learn?

If we do not listen, we are not likely to find out.

25
Funeral

19 July

Mr Demos is in hospital. He has suffered a heart attack.

The relief in those areas of the village subject to his bossy interference is almost tangible. I share it fully.

This unworthy reaction is reinforced by a circumstance typical of the Demos attitude to myself.

It was two days before the grapevine informed me that Mr Demos had been stricken. And, when I went to see Mrs Demos for news, she told me that I had not been informed on orders from her lord and master.

She said that he said: 'Don't bother the vicar. I'll be home again in a couple of days.'

A more probable version is: 'Don't tell the vicar. Let him find out for himself.'

I incline to the latter view because, when I did go to see him, he at once accused me of dereliction of duty. 'I've been here three whole days and you have only just got round to coming to see me.'

I swallowed my irritation as well as I might and made a few standard remarks. But he was not communicative and I was glad to come away, having made a mental note of his probable condition. There is no reason to suppose that this is very serious and the probability is that our respite from his attentions will be short-lived. He should be his horrible self again in two or three weeks' time.

I must be careful. Cedric is getting on his high horse. He says that it is one thing to work out how you will get on with one of your churchwardens out of action and quite another to wish the state of affairs to be permanent.

Suppose Mr Demos had another heart attack? Would I be glad? Suppose Mr Demos becomes a permanent invalid and was compelled to resign. Would we rejoice?

Suppose Mr Demos were to die…

A terrible thought presents itself. If Mr Demos died, I would have to conduct the funeral and deliver an oration. For it is the custom at Chilford to deliver an oration at funerals praising the deceased.

Sometimes it is a little difficult to be strictly honest. My relationship with Mr Demos would make it extremely difficult for me to be strictly honest.

Some of my clerical brethren dodge the issue by stating clearly, when they take over a parish, that they will never deliver funeral orations. I have missed the chance to make such a statement. And besides, in this case, Mr Demos has been an extremely prominent public character in Chilford for many years.

Some ignore the individuality of the deceased altogether and give a little sermon on salvation, death and resurrection. This may be very helpful in the case of humble and unobtrusive folk but quite inadequate in the case of Mr Demos.

It might be possible to cope. I once attended the funeral of an old curmudgeon who had been the terror of the place in which he lived. He had a smallholding and lived a hermit existence on it until anyone approached. Then his dogs were well trained to deal with them. If he was obliged to meet anyone by way of business, his extreme rudeness and awkwardness could be guaranteed.

At the funeral, his vicar performed miracles. Without uttering an untrue word, he managed to depict the old villain as a child of God whose loving father had now, in his mercy, removed him from this sinful world in which he had suffered so sorely for so many years.

Well, there is good in everyone and we clergy must be aware of it and make the most of it. But Mr Demos is still so much in my hair that I just cannot view his personality dispassionately. I am not so wicked as to wish him dead, of course, but I do wish he would get lost. If he goes to his reward during my incumbency, I shall be faced with frightful problems.

One day, someone will have to conduct my funeral. I wonder what he (or she) will say from the pulpit. It may be a kindness to leave strict instructions that there be no sermon. Let people think what they will without making a public meal of it.

26
Doom Watch

26 July

What is the world coming to?

Well, what? I do not know in any detail. Mrs Woollacombe does not know at all. Perhaps that is why she poses the question every time I see her.

Mrs Woollacombe is a lady in her mid-seventies, a widow of many years. I have never heard her speak of her husband but I have gathered from other sources that he was a shadowy figure of little consequence.

The only child of this union of long ago emigrated to Australia in his early twenties and, although his mother says she hears from him regularly, she never has any news to impart and, as far as is known, he never comes home to see her.

When Mrs Woollacombe speaks of her son, she glows. He was a lovely boy, she says, the model of what a son should be to his mother. Elderly residents who remember the lad are inclined to produce contrary opinions. But a mother should know best, even if her memory is selective and her mind given to fantasy.

After all, the boy's youth was spent in the good old days of long ago. And it is amazing how wonderful was the world, the country, the village of Chilford and Mrs Woollacombe's personal circumstances in the aftermath of the Second World War.

Hitler was defeated, the government was peopled with real politicians who had the welfare of the country at heart and everyone in Chilford worked together to make the village a happy place.

Not like today!

And if Mrs Woollacombe did not know what the world was coming to, she had no illusions about what it had come to so far.

The other day, I was served a large helping of her moanings. Apart from her standard strictures on modern youth, I can (happily) give no report on what she said. My mind wandered into the realms of more constructive thoughts.

In my more impatient moments I have thought that we clergy do waste a lot of our time sitting through these dreary monologues, which may go on and on and on. But one wiser than I has put it to me that the old and lonely are greatly helped by having a target for their depressing thoughts and that to have a listener is a kind of therapy, even if one's thoughts are entirely negative.

This is a comforting theory. It is difficult to love old Mrs Woollacombe as a vicar should, but he may be doing her a service by simply being there with a pair of ears, however inattentive.

Yet there must be some answer for those who believe that there is a God who has some sort of plan for the world. If Mrs Woollacombe's forebodings are correct, has his plan got totally out of hand?

To those of us who believe that the Bible covers all we are supposed to know about God and his workings, the book should surely give us some indication of what the world is coming to.

In fact, it does. But the message is not too comforting.

The outline of biblical prophesies on the subject is that, prior to the Day of Judgement and the setting up of God's Kingdom in victory over evil, we may expect such troubles in the world as would destroy everything and everybody, should not God intervene in time and save the good – those who remain faithful to the principle of God's love.

Conversations with Jehovah's Witnesses and the perusal of some of their writings indicate that they believe that the final time of terror is now upon us, and very soon now God will destroy the wicked and set up Christ's Kingdom on earth, though they give the impression that they alone are to benefit.

I doubt whether they have got the details quite right. For example, the Gospel states that the exact 'time of the end' is unknown to all but God himself and it is probable that he does not intend us to know precisely how the judgement and the coming of his Kingdom on earth are to come about.

We are told to be ready, that is all. We must strive here and now to develop and go on developing a loving relationship with God and our neighbours and trust the former to pull us through.

And that should be enough.

27
A Priest For Ever

2 August

The Reverend Basil Peabody has been at it again, lecturing us this time on the priesthood. How that little man does annoy me.

It seems that a certain Roman Catholic has told him that Anglican Holy Orders are not of God and so he is not validly ordained.

'And so I told him that the inclusion of Archbishop Parker in the first consecrations in Queen Elizabeth's reign guaranteed that our ordinations were valid and our priests true priests in the Apostolic Succession through the laying on of hands.'

We murmured something about 'teaching his grandmother to suck eggs'. We were all aware of the theory of the Apostolic Succession but doubted whether our congregations were much interested. We thought they wanted a man of God in the vicarage, one who could bring them spiritual nourishment. And that no amount of laying on of hands would guarantee that a priest was a good one.

'He has the power to celebrate the Holy Mysteries,' intoned Basil. 'His personal attributes are of no consequence.'

'You mean, then, that however badly you may behave, and whatever you may believe, you remain a true priest?'

'I mean just that,' said Basil with considerable satisfaction. 'As the Bible says, "You are a priest for ever".'

We forbore to point out that this was only half of the quotation in the Epistle to the Hebrews, and referred to Christ in any case. But it is useless to try arguing with Basil. He knows it all!

I expressed my displeasure concerning the bumptious Reverend Basil Peabody to the rural dean.

'I think we all feel as you do,' he said. 'It certainly worries me, though perhaps I do not get so worked up about it as I should.

'You probably don't know young Basil's history. He was the youngest, by several years, of a family of three, and his parents, I gather, scarcely bothered to hide the fact that his origin was the outcome of a slip-up in their birth control arrangements. In fact, he informed us that his father once told him outright that he was an unwanted child. That's hardly a good start in life is it?

'He was sent away to school, where he showed some academic ability but no athletic prowess. I do not fancy that he made many friends. Feeling a failure and unwanted, as we know, has a snowball effect and, by the time he was twelve or so, his inferiority complex was so advanced that he was fast becoming a problem child.

'And then a well-meaning master at his prep school took him in hand. The man evidently gave him every encouragement, which was good. He also urged him to assert himself and not care a damn about what other people thought of him, which was not so good.

'Accordingly, he pushed his way through public school and university, working hard and getting his degree but developing the opinionated and bombastic personality of which we are only too conscious.

'I do not know why he decided to be a priest. It may have been, as a friend of mine once put it, "more vestments than God". Or it may have been a mistaken effort to gain power over others. He is, as we know, extremely scrupulous about the details of Catholic ritual and order. This will give him a sense of security, and that, I imagine, is why he is so aggressive in his opinions and his self-importance. Really he is a very insecure person, very unsure of his faith and his relationships.'

I found this explanation helpful and it satisfied Cedric. I am now rather sorry for Basil, and a touch of compassion has diluted my irritation.

Nevertheless, I do hope he will overcome his distressing deficiencies. It seems to me that these sticklers for precise order in the priesthood who think they are all right with God if they perform the right rituals and say the right words at the right times distance themselves from their congregations and, too easily, from the Spirit of the Lord.

But maybe I am a bit of a sinner myself in that way.

28
But Nobody…

9 August

Some years ago I quoted, with approval, one of those Thirty-nine Articles of Religion set out in the 1662 *Book of Common Prayer*. These were written at a time when sectarian divisions in the Christian Church were perhaps more serious than they are today and the Anglican Church needed to state its position in matters of doctrine, especially as it concerned the Roman Catholics. In my youth, a newly appointed parish priest was required to read them from the pulpit and say that he 'assented' to them.

This 'assent' was one of those compromises so dear to the heart of Anglican comprehensiveness. One dared not say that, to be quite honest, you believed in them.

On the occasion of which I write I was quoting number twenty-three, which opens thus:

> It is not lawful for any man to take upon himself the office of public preaching or ministering the Sacraments in the congregation before he be lawfully called and sent to execute the same.

To me these sentiments seem exceedingly sensible. But my vis-à-vis was a young lady of progressive intellectual and theological pretensions who looked upon me with scorn and reduced me to dust with the words, 'But nobody nowadays believes in the Thirty-nine Articles.'

It was clear that my 'assent' to the articles was hopelessly out of date. Nobody, but nobody, took any notice of them in this enlightened age.

Recently I have reread the Thirty-nine Articles. They need an essay all to themselves. I may only say that there is an immense amount of sound sense in them. Meanwhile I am concerned with the state of mind behind the 'nobody nowadays' bit.

This young lady is a fairly extreme case of a common phenomenon, especially among young people with brains and a thoughtful approach to life that is not thoughtful enough. It is the belief that philosophy and culture are in a permanent state of progress towards Utopia, and this comes with the rider that anything thought to be new supersedes all that has gone before.

This in turn leads to contempt for tradition and the acquired wisdom of centuries, the rejection of authority and the fallacy that all intelligent people must agree with whatever 'new' and revolutionary doctrine happens to be popular at the moment.

Consequently, in the religious or theological circles that are my concern, we older and more experienced ministers are being told that 'nobody nowadays' believes in the Virgin Birth, the Resurrection, chastity or traditional morality of any kind. And that 'nobody nowadays' wants formal church services with moralising sermons.

I may be terribly conceited, but I must confess to a certain irritation at being labelled 'Nobody' by immature persons half my age.

The truth is that any philosophy of life, political, social or religious, needs three things: a firm aim founded on some immovable idealistic basis; lessons to be learned from history; and a set of principles by which we plan the future.

In a religious context, this means having a clear idea of whom or what we are really worshipping; what, in fact, is the most important thing in our lives. It means studying tradition in the light of history, seeing which theories have 'worked' to the benefit of mankind and why those that failed did not make the grade. It also means a sufficiently realistic view of human nature to influence the political, social and religious ideals of the future. Fallen human nature can fling large spanners in the works of so many bright ideas.

So many 'progressive' religious opinions are deficient in one or more of these ingredients.

Anyway, I am now too old to discard my fundamental beliefs and modernise myself to accommodate a younger, cleverer and more go-ahead (and inexperienced) generation. And if, in consequence, I am a has-been of no more use in the world, so be it.

But let me say a little bit to justify myself. I have thought about the big issues in life for far longer than have my young critics. Not only have I worked out good reasons for primitive laws, I have also learned the value of tradition and the emptiness of wholesale rebellion and any 'completely new start' advocated by contemporary fashion.

And, if 'nobody nowadays' believes in history, tradition, the Resurrection, sin, forgiveness, judgement, Hell, rules, moral standards, discipline and so on, then everyone must believe in chaos, anarchy and social mayhem.

On that basis I am content to be nobody.

29
Paranoid

16 August

Would that I had the wisdom of the serpent, for then I might have understood Annabel Marchbanks sooner and so remained as harmless as the proverbial dove in my dealings with her.

She was in her mid-thirties when I came to Chilford, married but childless. Her husband was not prominent and, although I have met him from time to time, he has never made much impression.

Annabel was a regular churchgoer and evidently a devoted Christian. She had been a nurse, was full of compassion for the suffering, and had a special concern for the mentally ill.

I never thought of her as one of the wolves who might cause any sort of upset, though occasionally she revealed a little flaw in her character. When crossed, she could react in a way quite out of proportion to the seriousness of the matter in dispute. Normally serene and friendly, there were moments when she appeared almost unbalanced.

We tended to gloss over these spasmodic incidents as being 'out of character'.

One day, when in an expansive mood, she told me of her ambitions. They were on the large side. She would never, she said, neglect her husband nor her domestic duties, but her real mission in life was to devote herself to the service of the mentally deranged.

'God is calling me,' she said, 'to be the Florence Nightingale of the mentally ill.'

I felt uncomfortable. Had she, I asked myself, anything like the force of character, the capacity for relentless hard work, the drive, the almost neurotic bullying power of that extraordinary woman to be able to fight for her objectives? And – perish the thought – was her 'call' really a delusion of grandeur?

I thought little more about Annabel's ambitions until fairly recently, when she asked me to send out a leaflet with the parish magazine. This advertised the formation of a religious movement she was inaugurating with a view to cherishing the mentally troubled. She would conduct quiet days in various places, where the troubled could come for meditation, religious exercise (yoga perhaps?) and counselling, all calculated to bring peace to the troubled mind.

I had some doubts as to whether she had the qualifications to bring such a move to fruition but, if this was God's call, who was I to question it? Anyway, I could see no harm in it, and I dispensed her leaflets.

The backlash came from young Mr James, one of our most loyal and dedicated Christians, who is not only a staunch pillar of the Church but a most reliable Christian witness in the parish.

He told me he had read Annabel's manifesto carefully and could see no mention of Christ, who was the true source of mental healing. This movement sounded to him too much like some form of New Age or cult worship. Could I find out more about it?

Perhaps I did not say the right thing. Perhaps I expressed myself badly. Perhaps I was too blunt. But I went to see Annabel and asked her whether her proposals were founded on prayer and whether she was consciously calling on the Holy Spirit for help in her healing work. Someone had pointed out that the information in her pamphlet read a little bit like cult propaganda, which could be very dangerous spiritually.

She was furiously angry.

'Who's saying that?' she demanded. 'I'm helping people. God has called me—'

I put my foot in it a bit deeper.

'No one doubts your motives,' I said as soothingly as I could. 'But often people do things with the best intentions without realising possible snags. New Age—'

'I know nothing about New Age,' she said. 'How could I be part of it?'

And she burst into tears.

I was shocked and again tried to stem the outburst.

'Don't talk to me,' she said. 'You're against me. Everyone's against me when I try to do good. You're absolutely devoid of Christian charity, all of you!'

I was reminded that 'being devoid of Christian charity' was one of her theme songs, always applied to others. She will never forgive me and she will never go to church again.

I might wait to hear Cedric's opinion but I think myself that Annabel is in need of a little healing herself before she can be of much help to others.

30
Not too Holy Baptism

23 August

There are a number of wolves on our new estate and one of them has been to fix a date for the baptism of a cub.

It is the female of the species who came but vixen I certainly may not call her. Her name is Elaine Graham and she is an attractive and friendly young lady. She explained that she is 'not very religious' but does think that a baby ought to be 'done'.

I agreed. But what about the child's father? I was careful not to say 'your husband', being aware of the domestic situation involved.

'Oh, Phil says that if it's OK by me, it's OK by him.'

I know Phil vaguely. If he is at home by chance when I call, he makes himself scarce. He looks to be a pleasant enough young man but I take it that he too is 'not very religious'.

I arranged a time when I would call and go over the baptism service with them, and I stressed that I meant 'them'!

Elaine departed and I sat down to face the theological problems involved, or some of them.

I normally conduct baptisms as part of the Family Communion though I have been stymied on that one because Aunt Mabel, or whoever, could not get there on time. I could not decide whether this would be appropriate for the present occasion, though I thought it probably would.

Anyway, I went to see the couple at the time appointed, presuming that there would be two or three godparents laid on, who would probably be also nice friendly young people, though 'not very religious'.

I was not expected but Phil happened to be around. He was dragged in out of the garden, where he had been depositing manure on the rhubarb. I turned off the television and we got down to business, more or less.

Thankfully, I was not treated to a reaction similar to that of the jolly friendly father who had said, on such an occasion some time previously, 'Let's leave God out of this, shall we, Vicar, and get on with the job?' Even so, it was clear that neither Phil nor Elaine had a clue what it was all about.

These, with two or three others like them, were informed that they were required to announce publicly that they believed and trusted in God, that they renounced evil and that they could guarantee to bring up their offspring in the fear and nurture of the Lord, or its modern equivalent.

They would really like to come to the Family Service for the baptism, but unfortunately the time had been chosen to coincide with baby's feeding time and so it must be 'private' at 3 p.m.

My problems multiplied. Was not their total absence of understanding and their perjured expressions of faith going to make a mockery of the whole business?

In such cases, some of my brother sheep refuse to cross the road into secular pastures. They will not baptise babies of unwed parents. They insist on a period of church attendance previous to the ceremony. And they will urge that they are being loyal to the Lord by so doing.

I would find this attitude very difficult to implement in practice. Phil and Elaine are such a friendly couple. They would agree to any little rules I proposed and then ignore them or find excuses for not complying. What does one do then? Cancel the arrangements and raise a stink in the parish? Or turn a blind eye and condone the perjury and the hypocrisy?

Pondering this problem, I dozed and dreamed.

I dreamed of three fat sheep contemplating a lost lamb. They were discussing which one would adopt the little one and care for it. The first declined because it had strayed from another flock and so was none of their business. The second said she knew its real parents and they were a bad lot. It would be better not to encourage the perpetuation of that strain. The third said it was a poor little beast anyway, and might just as well be left to die. Then the shepherd appeared, gathered up the lamb, and took it home. And so I awoke.

I conducted the baptism. The little wolf behaved very well, and I presented him to the Good Shepherd in my prayers. Maybe others did likewise. I wouldn't know.

And maybe, even if the parents and godparents are 'not very religious', the same Shepherd may get a word or two across to the cub through other channels.

Who am I to judge?

31

Nothing to Wear

30 August

No! I am not getting at Christine, who is always decently and sensibly clad without making any sort of fuss about her wardrobe. I refer quite generally to the cry that goes up in so many households when some important social event is looming and Mr and Mrs Porringer, or whoever, do not wish to go but think they ought to.

Mrs Porringer, if she must go, is determined to get the most out of it. She says: 'But I have nothing to wear!'

Assuming that Mr Porringer is a man of experience who has been well trained, he will pack her off to the most expensive ladies' outfitter in town with a blank cheque drawn on his account. If he is neither of these things, he may well point out that his wife's wardrobe is bursting with garments in all sorts of sizes, shapes and colours.

Mrs Porringer will then look at him pityingly. How could a man be so obtuse, so gauche? She explains that she possesses nothing suitable for that occasion.

If Mr Porringer is teachable, he will then understand that, if a lady is invited to a wedding, say, the first thing she must do is to buy a new hat and that other social invitations are accepted on the same principle.

But, even if there is something to wear, it is possible for persons of discernment to see through the most chaste, the most elegant of society chic. I recollect hearing an elderly preacher of the Spurgeon school fulminating against the Royal Ascot spectators, or some such. He referred to 'well-dressed women

[…] in rags before God'. Spurgeon, incidentally, was a forceful Victorian preacher who attracted large crowds. He advised other preachers to 'dangle his audience over the pit.' The Victorians evidently loved it.

What then are clothes really for? Why do we wear them at all, provided we may avoid the rigours of an English summer? Our more remote ancestors had literally nothing to wear and apparently felt no need of summoning the purveyors of lingerie until Eve got ideas into her head and the Good Lord ordered aprons.

The stated purpose was to 'hide their shame'. That probably suits most of us, apart from a few eccentrics and the ladies who pose for the more sensational newspapers and magazines, who evidently have nothing to wear. But presumably they have no shame, either.

Perhaps there is something symbolic about it all. There are certainly biblical references to being 'clothed with humility' and 'putting on the armour of righteousness', which have nothing to do with visits to Bond Street or Marks and Spencer.

Then, as Cedric is inclined to remind me, there may well be elements in our thoughts and actions that we prefer hidden from public scrutiny. We may well try to clothe them in forgetfulness, protestations of innocence or downright lying.

I agree that this sort of garment turns ragged and smelly if left on too long. It is essential for our souls' health that such clothes be removed before bathing in the love and forgiveness of God, but do let us do it in private.

The proper places to strip are the confessional or our own secret chamber with the door shut and the curtains drawn. Peeping Toms are not to be encouraged.

And that brings me to another thought, of which Cedric approves: he is always on to me about shedding the cloak of pretence and the armour of self-justification before God (who can see through them anyway). But he does insist that I disrobe in private, or possibly with the help of a close friend. We do not want others muscling in on the act. And I find it extremely distasteful when media hounds, whose cesspit minds are themselves clothed in smug hypocrisy, take it upon themselves to strip the famous in public.

It is even more nauseating when they tell us that the public 'has a right to know' what they find underneath. I eschew such a right, vigorously.

But it might be best if we did not feel the necessity to wear such garments, simply because we had nothing to hide.

32
Vicar's so Broad-minded

6 September

Our Women's Fellowship, as a change from the more serious matters of raising money for their own administration or running competitions for the prettiest pincushion, hold a party once a year, to which certain local dignitaries are invited. The vicar is one such dignitary.

I recently attended this year's effort. And, although Christine did warn me that there was to be an 'entertainer', there was no escape.

I can enjoy parties – I like a good meal – but the word 'entertainer' fills me with foreboding. Even a conjurer can cause anxiety, since a conjurer must keep talking.

This entertainer was commended because he had appeared on local television, though why that should commend him, I do not know. I have been sufficiently unfortunate in my time to hear TV comedians whose efforts have made me cringe with embarrassment, not on my account but on theirs.

I did my duty and attended the party. And in due course, after a very good meal, the entertainer took the stage.

For a moment he was put off by seeing a clerical collar in the audience, but only for a moment. He soon recovered and started his patter and it was not long before I heard the dreaded, doom-laden words: 'I know the vicar's broad-minded.'

There followed a series of 'jokes' of such a level of humour that I doubt whether a filthy-minded adolescent would have thought they made the grade.

I suppose that the presumption was that, should I not be

sufficiently 'broad-minded' to find this pathetic witlessness amusing, I would be shocked.

I was not amused, but neither was I shocked. I merely found it a tragic reflection on our society that a so-called comedian could be paid money to stand up and make such an appalling exhibition of himself.

On the face of it, it was perhaps more tragic that the ladies of our Fellowship could laugh at so much of it. It is perhaps charitable to assume that they were so caught up by the party spirit that anything would have kept them happy.

I was dragged into this incident by a feeling that it was my duty to attend parish functions. Some of my brethren are trapped into far worse situations by trying to be 'with it'.

I recollect one such who was persuaded to take part in a TV show. He was blindfolded and called upon to feel and identify an object of sex-shop merchandise. Either his compliance or his embarrassed silence was calculated to send the studio audience into raptures of merriment.

I sometimes wonder whether these background gigglers are given some sign by the producer to tell them when to turn on the laughter.

If being broad-minded means that we clergy are expected to approve of and enjoy obscenity, let me remain narrow-minded. And Cedric agrees.

In certain company we are apt to feel out of touch, remote and on a pedestal as it were. This is uncomfortable. But we must resist the temptation to forget that even the sleaziest minds among the wolves expect Christian ministers and clergy to set an example and live up to high moral standards. And they are right so to expect.

We may see how degradation of the vicar's office may occur. He is a remote being and we are a little nervous of him. And the Church over which he presides has the reputation of being a closed shop of righteous persons with out-of-date ideas.

It is argued, quite rightly, that the vicar should go out among his flock, meet them where they are, share their joys and sorrows and practise 'empathy'.

It is the next step that may lead to trouble. The vicar becomes so friendly, so compassionate, so understanding, so 'broad-minded' and so terrified of causing offence by moralising or talking religion that sin is condoned, worldly standards take over, the sheep the Good Shepherd has sent among the wolves to try to reconcile them to Himself are themselves devoured by materialistic unrighteousness and the Lord is betrayed.

33
Training the Cubs

13 September

I hope that relief has now come to a long-running worry of mine, though the damage done will probably be an indelible blot on local society for some time.

Mrs Cullompton, the headmistress of our local primary school, has resigned.

Put another way, the governors have managed to sack her, after a prolonged and not very polite correspondence with the education authorities.

Under Mr Starkey, her predecessor, the children were taught academic basics, good manners and the elements of traditional Christian philosophy. The results were, in the opinion of the general public, satisfactory, both academically and socially.

But the local authorities were not so pleased. We live in a progressive age (theoretically) and Mr Starkey's ideas were considered too hidebound and outmoded. When he retired they were quick to replace him with a new broom, one who would bring new life and enlightenment to the running of the school: Mrs Cullompton.

I never took to Mrs Cullompton. I decided at our first meeting that she was definitely one of the wolves. She could not help being physically unattractive, but there was more to it than that. When she outlined to me her plans for running the school, she sounded as though she were quoting from a textbook, and one from the Bertrand Russell school of thought. In my opinion, that gentleman's educational theories have been tried and found wanting years ago.

We have never heard her husband mentioned, nor learned what had become of him. I still wonder…

'You're not very nice about some of your parishioners, are you?' (This was Cedric).

'Don't interrupt!'

As I was saying, from the first I mistrusted Mrs Cullompton. I sensed that she was bogus. I soon became personally involved. During the Starkey regime, I had, at his invitation, gone into the school once a week to conduct an assembly: a couple of hymns, a suitable talk, Bible readings and prayers for the children. Mrs Cullompton hoped I would not mind, but these visits must now be discontinued. It was quite wrong to give children religious instruction. If they found, later on, that they needed a religion, they could choose for themselves which one to adopt.

I held my peace. But I thought of those I knew who, brought up on that principle, had found it quite impossible to choose the religion that suited them because they had no idea on which to base their choice.

She started by telling the children that she was their new friend, who would never give them orders nor punish them. They were free to make use of any of the amenities offered or join any class they felt like joining, all when and where they chose. They were to be free and happy and she hoped they would call her Griselda.

In theory, there were rewards for good attendance at classes but since no child must be humiliated by failure, these were distributed wholesale and accepted as of right. I was not surprised that Mrs Cullompton had staff problems from the start.

True religious instruction was not optional because it did not exist. But there were substitutes to choose from. There were lectures on racism, Green Peace, world poverty and homelessness, pacifism and so on. And children who were moved to attend picked up a number of subversive political slogans of whose import they had little appreciation.

Utopia did not materialise. Children who wanted to learn were unable to do so, owing to the chaos and hubbub going on around them. And children who did not want to learn became utterly bored with nothing positive to do. Even the fun of being disruptive palls in time.

Somehow, none of them ever learned that Mrs Cullompton was their friend. They called her 'Grizzly' or 'Grizzly Bear' and despised her.

And most of them hated school. I once told the woman that young children wanted to be given definite standards, that they enjoyed discipline fairly applied and normally accepted punishment without rancour if they knew it was just.

She thought I was crazy.

'Freedom,' she snapped, 'brings out the best in them!'

'And the worst,' I said. I could not help it.

I am sorry for her now she has gone. She is a desperately lonely person led astray by false teaching and misguided philosophies.

She must have longed for those children to love her.

34
Why so Sad?

20 September

I'm depressed again. This happens from time to time, and too frequently. Am I a manic depressive? Perish the thought. Certainly not me. It would offend my pride terribly to own that I may be mentally ill.

Whether ill or not, I have these fits of depression, and I don't know why. Christine, bless her, is anxious and makes soothing noises. But, when she asks what ails me, I say I am OK, simply because I cannot articulate my feelings.

There should be no cause for this state of affairs. Christine is a great support, and our son is doing well. I have no domestic tensions.

There is not quite the same euphoria in the parish as at first, but that is routine. 'The honeymoon is over' is the way it is usually expressed. It is nothing serious.

The church is well attended and well run. There is a good supply of capable and reliable church workers and a flourishing Sunday school. We even have some regular and faithful teenagers.

The Demos disease is in remission. Apart from the fact that the man is on holiday, his mind has evidently been on other things recently. In church circles, he has been far less aggressive. Long may it last.

Nevertheless, there is something bugging me all the time, and I think I know what it is.

The ordained ministry is a calling and we priests are called to the service of God. The service of mankind is an essential outcome of serving God, but it is not a substitute for it. Our task is to preach, teach and heal in Christ's name, which means in his Spirit. In other words, we are called to lead our flocks into reconciliation with God and so extend his Kingdom of Love.

The intended result is the building up of a community of men and women who, primarily, love the Lord their God and so bring forth among us the fruits of the Spirit: love, joy, peace and so on.

It is not happening. There must be something wrong with the theory or the practice. Is it the fault of the sheep or the wolves?

This particular sheep has always taken evangelism seriously enough to believe that his aim is the conversion of the wolves. When no such conversion is apparent, he should first examine himself.

It is no false pride to say that this sheep is among those who do love God in that he lives close to him, believes in his revealed word and entrusts his thoughts and aspirations to him for correction or censorship. He honestly tries to obey him. But, since obedience involves loving one's neighbour as oneself there is scope for hesitation. One's love is terribly full of holes.

One point to the wolves.

Cedric agrees. He would!

On the other hand, many of the wolves are not exactly high on the ladder of sanctity, nor, apparently, do they wish to be.

There is plenty of support among them for good works, but not too much enthusiasm for those good works that are specifically and obviously of God.

Most people believe in God in a vague sort of way and there is little actual hostility. There is not much enthusiasm either.

Our church is much appreciated as a local shrine but not so much, consciously, as the house of God.

In obedience to the Lord's instructions to preach the gospel to every creature and knowing that so many are woefully ignorant of their faith, I recently circulated every house in the parish, all of whom receive personal visits at intervals, with a statement of Christian fundamentals. There was no comeback in word or deed.

There is, in fact, very little response to the work I was called and ordained to do and there are times when I feel reluctant and unwanted.

This is one of these times and this is what is bugging me.

'Suppose,' says Cedric, 'you spare us this orgy of self-pity and get on with the job, whether, as Ezekiel says, people pay attention or whether they do not. And trust the Lord, who said you must die to live, and lose to gain.

'Careful study of your aims, fallen human nature and the machinations of the Great Deceiver might help.'

35
Youth Club

27 September

I have been to have a look at the local youth club, where the teenage wolves gather once a week. Though now run entirely by the secular arm, it was founded by the Church and still congregates in the church hall.

Things were going quite well. The billiards and table tennis tables were occupied, a couple were playing darts and there was regular attendance at the canteen.

Several members were just sitting round talking and I noticed one couple whose intimacy had gone a bit beyond the conversational level, though it would be an unworthy exaggeration to introduce such words as 'necking' or 'snogging' or whatever modern vocabulary provides.

The perpetual thump, thump, thump issued from the record player, grossly but, as I am informed, necessarily magnified almost past bearing by the amplifier and loudspeakers.

The marvels of science are a mixed blessing.

I stayed about twenty minutes talking to (or shouting at) the bright young enthusiasts who run the show. Nobody else took any notice of us.

In my young days at theological college, our principal told us that we should refuse to do anything in our parishes that was not directly part of our proper work of promoting the Kingdom of God.

In my first curacy, I had no option. Whether or not the youth club had anything to do with the Kingdom of God, it was part of the curate's job to attend and mix with the kids. This, I found, was valuable. I got to know them better and got on well with many of them.

When I became vicar of Chilford and was asked to start a youth club, I made it a condition of membership that the youth attended half an hour of Bible study and discussion first.

Had I held everything in the vicarage, this move might have borne some fruit. In the church hall, it hardly registered. A handful, already churchgoers, attended the preliminary half-hour. The rest ignored it. And somehow it was not on to shut the doors on them for the subsequent games and social.

I had other ideas. Let the youth run their own club. Let them appoint a committee, secretary, treasurer, and one to organise games, discussion groups and competitions. They might even raise a football team. It would give them a sense of responsibility.

There was considerable unspoken opposition to this idea. One or two volunteers ran the canteen, but the young wolves generally did not wish to take on any responsibility. Nor did they wish to be organised. Games and entertainment must be laid on if they happened to be wanted, but club night was really a meeting place for friends. I saw no harm in that, though I did not see it specifically as a church matter for which I must be responsible.

I had to find adult helpers. Two offered: a young man and a young woman. They were 'good with youth' and very suitable for the job. But they were not churchgoers and the man was definitely hostile to organised religion though he had a well-developed social conscience.

He was quite happy that the Church should provide a meeting place for the club but, when I suggested that we held a youth service one Sunday, encouraging the club to attend and take part, he was positively rude about 'forcing people to go to church.'

The arrow was off target, but it hardly encouraged cooperation.

The original idea of combining club and Bible study had vanished long since. Now the club was no church organisation in any real sense.

Meanwhile, old Mrs Weston tells me that a youth club is good, because 'it keeps the young people off the streets'. I question the significance of this opinion. Our young folk are not thieves or muggers and there is little difference between their meeting on the streets or on club premises. Apart from that, some members spend part of club time making the environment hideous by racing around on their motorbikes.

And, some time ago, a certain girl produced an infant with the necessary cooperation of the North boy. They had become friendly at the club. And though the child's brief existence was not inaugurated on club premises, it was certainly not conceived on the streets.

To conclude, I would mention a fellow sheep who runs a very successful Bible class for interested teenagers. It has no connection whatever with fun and games. I conclude that Christ does not win youth by keeping them amused.

36
The Seat of the Scornful

4 October

I have always been a very well-behaved person with no vices. From my earliest youth I have subscribed to puritan standards of morality. I have shunned tobacco, alcohol and drugs, came virgin to marriage and have been faithful to Christine ever since. I am honest in all my dealings. I pay promptly what I owe, and make no efforts to beat the taxman. I am reasonably generous, and give a tithe of my income to charity.

I also fall headlong into the snares the devil prepares for such pillars of rectitude. The essence of the resulting temptation is to sit in judgement on those who live without any halo. And, unless I am very careful, all such may come under the umbrella of my censorious tongue. The trouble is that it is so satisfying to sit in an easy chair with the newspaper reading about murderers, thieves and adulterers and saying, 'I'm not a bit like that.' It gives one a real thrill to watch the TV news with its saga of horror and cruelty and mayhem and be able to say, 'That's just not my scene.'

I was voicing these thoughts the other day when Christine – backed up as usual by Cedric – suddenly said, 'You know, if Christ's tale of the Pharisee and the publican praying in the Temple were to be dramatised, you would be tailor-made for the title role. You would not even have to act.'

I was most indignant, especially as I knew that she had hit the bullseye. Even so, she need not have driven it home when I found her mending my trousers and referring to them as the 'seat of the scornful'.

I demanded an explanation, and got one.

'You ought to know what I mean,' she said. 'You are frightfully conscientious about going to church every morning to recite your daily office. And the very first verse you read in the psalms on the first day of every month puts it all very clearly.'

I did have the grace to look it up:

> Blessed is the man that hath not walked in the counsel of the ungodly, nor stood in the way of sinners, *nor sat in the seat of the scornful* [...]

If domestic relations in the vicarage are slightly strained at present it is because Christine is knocking me; she is dead right and I do not like it.

As for Psalm One, it starts off all right, but that second part of the first verse (my italics) can be a hearty slap in the face.

I tried arguing with Cedric.

I said, 'What then? Am I to condone sin? Am I to pretend that sinners do no harm in the world and that their moral failings do not matter? Am I to find excuses for all the evil that men do and leave it at that?'

But Cedric would not wear it.

He said, 'Don't be childish. There is a world of difference between denouncing sin and sneering at sinners. There is a huge gap between pointing out that sin has evil consequences and rejoicing when a sinner receives the just reward of his deeds. You can face up to failure in others without adopting a priggish "holier-than-thou" attitude. You can read on to verse two: "His delight is in the law of the Lord." And,' said Cedric, 'the law of the Lord is love.'

I must agree that the implications and the working out of love in our attitudes and relationships would be a good Lenten penance. It would take hours. And if it involves adding humility to one's many virtues, well, don't let's boast about it.

37
What am I Worth?

11 October

I'm at it again.

I have spent the afternoon of a day-off sitting in the sun, contemplating my financial virtues. It has been exceedingly agreeable.

I am a very honest man. I would not, of course, wish to boast about it in a naughty world, but there it is. It is a simple matter of fact.

I loathe owing money. It makes me feel unclean. I insist on paying for things at the moment of purchase, or as soon as the bill comes in. I do not use credit cards, nor will I indulge in hire purchase activities.

The last people with whom I do business are the wolves who advertise their merchandise on television with the slogan, 'No deposit – start paying next April' or those who mark their goods 'Only £19.99' when they mean £20 and worth about half.

Unlike some wolves, I am not concerned with 'getting away with' anything. If I receive goods or services to which a price is attached, I like to pay for them, and quickly.

On no account would I borrow money from a friend to meet personal wants. Nor, incidentally, am I anxious to lend for the same reason in others. All should live up to my standards and my friends should not be encouraged down the paths of debt and prodigality.

You will observe, I hope, that I am not being self-righteous, merely stating facts.

I take a dim view of those who are perfectly able to pay their taxes, community charges and so forth but refuse to do so on some personal principle. And I take a dimmer view of those of my fellow sheep who discourage their PCCs from paying the church quotas for the same reason.

The authorities will get their money. And if I refuse to pay my share, someone else will foot the bill.

I am really very considerate, am I not? Some people must think I'm awfully stuffy and ridiculously pompous. I care not what they think. In this frame of mind I have faced the matter of 'vicar's expenses'.

The principle laid down from on high proclaims that our poor underpaid clergy should have all their expenses of office met by the PCC, in addition to having a free house with half the rates excused and the other half paid by the parish.

This is a rash directive, since it is wide open to abuse. It gets it from those of my fellow sheep who define 'expenses of office' with extreme liberality in their own favour.

I scorn such sheep in my heart. I am so scrupulously honest myself about assessing my expenses of office that I go further and ask myself whether I am doing my job sufficiently conscientiously to deserve such perks.

This is where I have come unstuck.

I have just heard that Mr Demos has held a secret meeting with two or three cronies to discuss my expenses. He says (or so I am reliably informed), 'Before the PCC sanctions these expenses, we should consider whether the vicar deserves what he is asking for.'

I am absolutely furious. The sheer insolence of the man! Who does he think he is to pass judgement on my work? Let the conceited old gasbag look to his own behaviour. Is he worth his salary, whatever that may be?

Cedric butts in. 'What a way to talk about one of your parishioners!'

'Shut up, Cedric.'

'I won't shut up! You must love your neighbours and Mr Demos is your neighbour.'

It will take another sunny afternoon to work out the implications of that terrible thought.

38
Isn't it Awful?

18 October

What fun it must be to be a journalist or a radio newscaster. It should be most satisfying to feed the eyes and ears of the great British public with an endless catalogue of crime, violence, scandal, horror and despair.

Twice I have seen it suggested that all television news programmes should, as a matter of principle, contain one item of good news. And twice have I seen the suggestion dismissed out of hand as being unrealistic.

'Unrealistic' in this context means, presumably, unwanted or 'not commercial'. If so, it has a point. For, by some strange quirk of human nature, most of us enjoy bad news.

From time to time, I visit Wilfred Charlesworth. He is a retired professional man in his late sixties. He has had a successful business career and inhabits a very nice house with a well-kept garden that he loves. His wife of forty years is a delightful woman and they have two grown-up sons, both happily married and doing well in their respective careers. There are four grandchildren who should give them great pleasure.

Mr Charlesworth is in good health, is a regular churchman and has many interests. His main interest is world affairs and that is perhaps where he comes unstuck. For he is a real moaner. The international scene, the hopeless incompetence (and chicanery) of the government and the morals of youth – you name it – all contribute to an outlook of unrelieved gloom.

I have seen Mrs Charlesworth attempt to soothe him with the presentation of the 'bright side', but he will have none of it.

'Things are bad,' he said, 'and it's no use pretending otherwise.'

He might as well have said, 'I'm determined to be thoroughly miserable, and nobody's going to stop me.'

I have a distant cousin, a lady who is the life and soul of her social set in the little country town she inhabits. On most mornings, some half a dozen worthy vixens meet for coffee in the local tearoom.

There they tear to shreds the reputations of their neighbours, my cousin being the most savage. I have been present once or twice and been quite appalled at the gratuitous shockers that have passed their lips.

The interesting thing is that these ladies have no personal grudge against those they are slandering. Their motive is the sheer joy of character assassination. For whatever reason, many of us enjoy the miserable and love scandal.

And so, to return to television, we sit glued to the news, or the dreary 'real' world of the soaps. Spasmodic comments burst from our lips: 'Isn't it dreadful?' 'Isn't she horrible?' 'It's just one disaster after another,' 'I can hardly bear to watch it.' And so on.

It is sometimes suggested that, should we find television too utterly depressing, watching is not compulsory and we can always turn the thing off.

But that would never do. Nothing must deprive us of our daily ration of horror, scandal and disgust.

I find this all a bit difficult to accept because it is my job to preach the gospel of Christ and 'gospel' means 'good news'.

And so it is. Once a Christian has surrendered to his Lord and has agreed to serve him on his terms, he comes to the state of Saint Paul, who had a very rough life but knew that nothing – but *nothing* – could separate him from the love of God in Jesus Christ.

It is good news to know that the risen Christ loves us, lives in us and can inspire us to conquer evil in our own lives.

It is good news to know that Sue Chamberlain who does such wonderful work with handicapped children and is such a cheerful and inspiring person, lives in Chilford as well as Mr Charlesworth.

It is good news that we have young Mr James, who has the temerity to stand up to and counteract Mr Demos.

And there are all those others in the parish whose lives and relationships reflect the Spirit of God, shining through nature, art and human nature and bringing lasting joy and security to many.

But then, of course, acceptance of the joys of life would deprive us of the pleasures of being miserable.

39
Meet Me Where You Are

25 October

In my earnest and idealistic youth, I pictured a parish priest as a shepherd preaching the gospel and leading his sheep into the ways of righteousness and peace.

The sheep, craving spiritual nourishment, had only to be told and they would flock to listen to the wisdom pouring from his lips.

How could I have been so naive? As a fox will kill without eating, so will a wolf go ego-boosting by destroying the gospel without drawing from it any nourishment whatsoever.

It was soon brought home to me that people were just not flocking to church to gather up the pearls of my preaching. Many of them, though friendly enough, regarded the church as a building without spiritual significance, which had to be kept going because there was a vague something about it. This at best. At worst it was just a ghetto for the self-righteous.

Most of us were agreed that, if the church did not attract people, then it must go out to the people.

Very right and proper. I have always been a good visitor and found the practice very valuable in terms of building good relationships. Yet 'meeting people where they are,' mentally and spiritually, is not always a simple matter.

The trouble is that, although wolves are gregarious animals, their mental equipment is surprisingly individual, and 'meeting them where they are' leads you into a multitude of different places.

One will tell you he is an atheist, another an agnostic, others

Muslims, Hindus, Jehovah's Witnesses, New Agers or whatever. Or simply that they 'have the right' to make up their own religion, and don't want yours 'thrust down their throats'.

Some live in a world where Christianity is just a matter of being kind to other people, or being 'saved' without defining that process. Some find charismatics unacceptable and vice versa. Some are staunch adherents of the social gospel. Some are pantheists.

All seem agreed on one thing: that of course the vicar would go along with their point of view and they would 'never go to church again' if he upset them in any way.

This is an empty threat indeed in some cases.

Added to these variations are those on the offensive who tell the vicar what he ought to be doing and where he gets off if he is not doing it. He must hold study groups, run youth clubs, make the services more attractive and hold them at more suitable times and 'be on our side' in any disagreement.

It is comparatively easy to meet all these good people 'where they are'. But where, if anywhere, do you go from there?

Once again, Cedric tells me to cool down and think of all those good church people who are building a community of real Christian believers seeking the love of God.

'Sometimes,' he says, 'you get positively paranoid in your generalisations about those who don't go along with you'.

All right then. Ignoring Mr Demos, I am determined to meet my parishioners where they are, but in love.

I am a conscientious man and I take seriously the instruction that bids me say matins and evensong 'on behalf of the parish' in church, ringing the bell to announce the fact.

Normally, this is a routine procedure, but sometimes a passage of scripture, even if well known, leaps from the page and hits you in the face with new force.

This happened to me the other day.

Exodus chapter 34 tells of God's instructions to the wandering Israelites. They are to meet the Canaanites where they are, in order to conquer them and probably make slaves of them. They are not to fraternise. They are to destroy their religious culture. What wicked, racist, pro-apartheid and anti-Christian orders are these?

Quite. But there was a reason for them. If they fraternised with the Canaanites, the primitive Israelites would probably be compromised by adopting their pagan beliefs and practices.

Jesus did 'meet people where they are' and was criticised accordingly. But his supreme spiritual maturity forbade any possibility of his being adversely influenced by them. He came down to man in order to bring man up to God.

We sheep are weaker vessels, mentally and spiritually. We have watered down, distorted or 'improved on' the Christian faith to suit modern man to such an extent that even the clergy, who should know better, 'meet people where they are' and are compromised by or even wholeheartedly adopt a lot of their pagan and anti-Christian beliefs and morals.

40
Outing

1 November

It is the tradition in most villages that any organisation has a Christmas party and an annual outing.

Chilford is no exception and I have recently endured the annual outing of the Chilford Women's Fellowship.

There are some twenty-five members of this important body. It was founded several years ago by Mrs Worthington and is still run by her.

It is Mrs Worthington's nature to run things and the Women's Fellowship is run strictly in accordance with her wishes. The annual outing follows the programme she has laid down.

The outing has to last as long as possible because Mrs Worthington must have value for money. We congregate at 9 a.m. and expect to be home by 11 p.m. How she gets round the rules governing working hours for coach drivers I do not know.

The age range starts at about forty. Some half a dozen members are definitely elderly, with attendant infirmities, and Mrs Crabtree has turned ninety.

The busload is made up with husbands and a few others who are willing to pay the fare. Christine is a member. I am an honoured guest by virtue of my office. I insist, though, on paying my way, to the considerable annoyance of Mrs Worthington.

In early days, there was a problem of people booking a place on the coach and not turning up. Now we pay when we book and the charge is not returnable.

The present problem is created by Miss Rufflet and Mrs Moloney. Owing to some personal fracas of long, long ago, Miss

Rufflet enjoys a vicious hatred of Mrs Moloney. Miss Rufflet is a member of the Fellowship; Mrs Moloney is not. But Mrs Moloney does enjoy an outing and enhances her pleasure with the knowledge that her presence will drive Miss Rufflet to madness.

They are placed as far as possible apart on the bus since Mrs Worthington realises that their joint company almost makes 'fellowship' a dirty word.

Old Mrs Haliburton creates a minor problem. She is a compulsive talker and the sole topic of her conversation is Old Mrs Haliburton. This is a subject of no interest to anyone else and if, by divine providence, there are any spare seats on the bus, one will be found next to Mrs Haliburton.

On this occasion we took to the road at 9.30 a.m. The morning passed pleasantly enough and it was only lunchtime that heralded our day of discontent.

Mrs Worthington had booked a meal for us on the recommendation of a friend. The arrangements were made by telephone and no reconnoitring had been undertaken.

The room prepared for us was upstairs and very steep stairs they were. The toilet arrangements were badly placed and quite inadequate for a large party of women. Old Mrs Crabtree had no problems; her vitality is inexhaustible and she was determined to enjoy herself. The more infirm elderly had considerable difficulties.

Owing to poor communication, some of us did not get what we ordered and the service was poor. Discontent mounted.

We moved on to our main objective: a small cathedral city crammed with buildings and places of historical and architectural interest. We were let loose for three hours to look round. Unhappily, only two or three of the party were even faintly interested in places of historical and architectural note. They only wanted to look at the shops, and it was early closing day, rigidly observed.

By 5 p.m. most of us were fed up and longed to get home. But this was impossible. The coach had been booked until 11 p.m. and home was less than two hours' journey away. We moved on to Belhampton, a little market town that went fast asleep at about

7 p.m. and there the tedious hours ticked slowly away.

Two or three men went to the pub but, generally speaking, pubs were not our scene. It was now raining, so we stayed in the coach.

Only Mrs Worthington and Mrs Crabtree showed much sign of being alive. Merciful slumber overtook a very few but for most the dead hand of utter boredom descended like a blanket.

Shortly after 8 p.m. Mrs Worthington agreed to call it a day. But then Mrs Haliburton was missing. She turned up, wet through, at 9.20 p.m.

We reached Chilford at 11 p.m., exhausted with boredom. Only Mrs Worthington maintained that we had had a good day.

After all, we did get our money's worth.

41
PCC

8 November

To quote Groucho Marx (I think), 'I have had a very pleasant evening – but this was not it.'

I have been to a meeting of the Parochial Church Council. In past days, these meetings have been friendly and productive affairs. Of course, we have had our moments of waffle, postponing decisions, continuing to argue about matters when a vote has been taken and the motion decided by a majority and, no doubt, the usual informal continuation of the meeting on the pavement afterwards. But the brouhaha used to be quite amicable and we were, I believe, genuinely concerned about the welfare of the Church and not so much about our own little egos, even if we disagreed about the best way the welfare of the Church was to be implemented.

But things have changed as Mr Demos' delusions of omniscience and omnipotence have grown in line with his personal hostility to myself.

Tonight there was a crisis.

It was a matter of money.

I have always hated discussing money in Church affairs. It rouses the worst in so many human breasts and may easily reinforce the image of the Church as a pretty worthless institution, always on the grab.

To avoid this slander I tried to hide behind Jesus' command with promise: 'Seek ye first the Kingdom of Heaven, and all these things will be added unto you'.

I interpret this to mean that, if the Church devoted its energies towards doing its job of preaching God's word and doing his work in the world, the necessary funds would come rolling in from grateful well-wishers.

The catch is in that word 'first'. For, in a church living under the iron dominance of Mr Demos, church organisation and management with their attendant funds come first, and spiritual work fits in as best it may.

I try to ignore this by insisting that no pressure is put on anyone to give money to the church. We have a plate for offertory and do not pass a bag round. There is an envelope scheme and a covenant scheme for those who want it. And there are the usual boxes at the back of the church for donations and the sale of cards, books and so forth.

I publish, in the magazine, the church's needs but I will certainly not tell anyone what I think they ought to give.

Tonight I was under pressure because the diocese has butted in with a special appeal. Careful survey has revealed that Bilchester Cathedral is in a pretty horrific state of disrepair. Millions of pounds are required, much of it urgently. 'We ask that every parish appeals to all parishioners to protect their great architectural heritage,' and so on.

I doubt whether more than ten per cent of our wolves care much whether our cathedral stands or falls, but one must do one's best.

I suggested a contribution from church funds.

'That,' said Mr Demos, 'is not appealing to everyone'.

'An envelope to every house to be collected?'

'You promised, Vicar, that you would never do that,' said Mr Demos, his voice charged with acid. 'And everyone is sick of these appeals, anyway.'

'A special box in the church for contributions?'

'Money raised in our church is for our church,' said Mr Demos. 'It's not to be squandered on any tinpot scheme that turns up.'

Aware that the man was being awkward deliberately (or bloody-minded, as I said to myself), I made my first error.

'How then do you propose to launch this appeal?' I asked angrily.

Mr Demos remained infuriatingly calm.

'I don't propose it at all,' he said. 'It's your duty to decide these matters.'

I made my second error. I completely lost my temper.

'And it's yours,' I almost shouted, 'to back me up! How can a church function properly if a churchwarden rejects everything the vicar says or does?'

'A churchwarden,' said Mr Demos rudely, 'knows his parish. And it is his duty to see that an incompetent vicar knows what people want and prevent his making a fool of himself.'

And, without a word of apology, he got up and left the meeting. After a few moments of stunned silence, I made my third error.

'I see no point in my carrying on,' I said, 'if my authority is slighted in this fashion. I declare this meeting closed'.

And I too walked out.

I suppose we shall get over it. At present I am too furious with Demos to think clearly and too angry with myself for not handling it better.

42
Remorse

15 November

We have survived last week's PCC meeting and I have called another to deal with the business then left undone. I am not looking forward to it. The whole atmosphere is now wrong, and my flare-up last week has not improved matters.

Mr Demos has not apologised. I never expected he would. Nor can I bring myself to apologise to him, though Cedric tells me that I am in part to blame. I feel too sore.

A church meeting, more than any other public meeting, should be a gathering where matters may be discussed in a friendly and cooperative attitude without personalities intruding into the business. It becomes quite intolerable if one member spends all his or her time being bitchy.

Mr Demos is motivated entirely by self-importance and dislike or envy of myself. If he or anyone else sees difficulties or objections to what is proposed of course they should say so, but what they say may be chewed over and submitted to the chairman for final judgement. Personal opposition to the chairman is quite unnecessary and does much harm. With us at the moment, it is making church business impossible.

And if a vicar's authority is not accepted by his church committee, nothing gets done, because business descends to the level of a cat fight.

'Stop moaning,' (this from Cedric) 'and let's hear a bit about the good dedicated Christians you have on your PCC.'

Very well. Most of them *are* good, public-spirited people who serve church and parish faithfully without throwing their weight around. Why, I ask, do they not back me up against this super-menace of a churchwarden who is such a thorn in my side? I know I am well liked in the parish and that Mr Demos, in spite of his conviction to the contrary, is extremely unpopular.

Part of the answer is that they are afraid of Mr Demos and they are not afraid of me. More than that, most of them hate these personal squabbles and distance themselves from them, for the sake of a peace that constantly eludes us.

We have another churchwarden, a quite amiable man who gets on with the job while Mr Demos does all the shouting. People like him but, under the shadow of his fellow warden, he is rather taken for granted and remains unnoticed.

Meanwhile, Mr Demos is re-elected year after year because nobody else wants the job.

One must, I suppose, look on the bright side. No one lasts for ever and one day there will have to be a successor to Mr Demos. There are one or two up-and-coming younger men and women of sterling worth who may, one day, bring the Christian spirit in to run our church affairs.

'That's enough about other people,' (Cedric again). 'Where do you stand in these matters? Why don't you control the situation better?'

Well, yes. I am ashamed that I lost my cool last week. The best way of dealing with the Demoses of this world, who are only out to get you, is to agree amiably with everything they say and then take not a blind bit of notice of it. When people are spoiling for a fight, nothing infuriates them more than to have the enemy ignore their existence.

In Gandhi's code, passive resistance may be much more effective than open warfare.

Nevertheless, that broadside about incompetent priests and the churchwarden's job being to prevent them making fools of themselves rankles. I must think it through.

As Cedric keeps reminding me, a little introspection now and again is quite in order and I must sit down and work out, calmly, my problems. Why am I not a stronger leader, who inspires confidence? Why can I not deflate Demos and control Chilford church?

Jesus was the supreme exponent of the art. No one got the better of him until 'his hour came' and his degradation at the hands of the power of evil was a necessary part of our salvation.

We Christians feed on his spirit. Perhaps one day I may be so filled with that spirit that I may control things better.

But I will not do it by getting mad.

43

The Lore and the Profits

22 November

At last! The Reverend Basil Peabody has come to grief. Time was when I would have rejoiced that the Church was shot of him but, having heard his history, I am a little bit sorry for him.

But he just would not learn.

He revealed at a chapter meeting the process by which he eventually fell from grace. We were discussing wisdom and most of us found biblical wisdom very difficult to define. The rural dean expressed the opinion that wisdom was essentially the word of God, a sort of mental and spiritual know-how that became incarnate in Jesus Christ.

Naturally, Basil knew better. He could define anything by the simple expedient of twisting it to conform to his personal outlook, which was 'forward-looking'. He told us that wisdom, or 'lore' as he called it, was progressive and was simply the most recent thinking of 'intelligent and unprejudiced' people.

'Lore', he explained, was the word to use for the pronouncements of prophets, ancient or modern and modern lore was continually superseding ancient lore.

Basil's whole philosophy is founded on a very popular modern heresy, namely that Man is the supreme arbiter of his own fate and has the right to decide the beliefs and moral codes that suit him.

In the context of the Christian religion, this usually leads to disbelief in the divinity of Christ and the acceptance of him solely as a 'man of like passions with ourselves'.

Basil never believed in miracles. To him, they were either

misinterpreted tales of events that witnesses could not understand or fictions created by the disciples to boost the reputation of their hero.

Anything recorded of Jesus that Basil could not understand, or was not in agreement with his own philosophy, was either a later addition to the text (so rendering it untrustworthy) or a sign of the primitive (and so valueless) outlook of the writer.

He conceded that Jesus was a very good man who was very badly treated. His crucifixion was an appalling miscarriage of justice. And, though Basil was very dubious about an afterlife, he was gracious enough to maintain that 'there might be some truth in it'. But nobody nowadays really believes in the Resurrection of Jesus and, though he might live on in the spirit world (if there was one), his position there was no different from that of any other martyr who has died for his faith.

From these beliefs, it was but a short step to imagine all the things about Jesus that might have been true, though never reported. And Basil approved very strongly of all those playwrights who, while making no pretence of being Christians themselves, were so 'honest' that they depicted Jesus as a superstar, a dervish, a religious fanatic of wild appearance and manner, or simply a Peeping Tom spying on Mary Magdalene with whom he was 'in love'. In Basil's view, all these misrepresentations helped to make Jesus 'more human'.

One thing poor Basil never learned: if a Christian rejects Christian standards and starts compromising with those of the world, the latter soon take over. And, for example, the dictum (true in itself) that 'sex is the gift of God' soon led Basil to accept that fornication, adultery, homoerotic practice and suchlike could all be expressions of God's love.

It soon became known that the young lady who attended the vicarage to clean and prepare meals had other duties to perform. Then he decided that his church treasurer was incompetent. Having a certain expertise in bookkeeping, he took on the job himself and it was not long before he found it personally profitable to keep the books on his own system.

Sex and finance eventually gained him press notoriety and the withdrawal of his licence by the bishop. He may be taken on somewhere else by the lunatic fringe but, for the sake of the Church, I hope not.

What profit did he hope to gain? Status? Advancement? The approval of intellectuals? The admiration of pagans? Perhaps he never rationalised his motives.

I only hope he may learn the import of the Lord's words: 'What does it profit a man if he gains the whole world and loses his own soul?'

44
Peace be with You

29 November

I am in an irreverent mood. I have just attended a church where they make a meal of the Peace.

The celebrant came to the chancel steps, flung wide his arms and said: 'The Peace of the Lord be always with you,' and a large congregation responded, 'And also with you'. All according to the book.

Then the whole community erupted into a positive banquet of Peace. It was almost an orgy. Some participants seemed too embarrassed to eat much but the majority turned to their neighbours, stretched over to touch others or walked about the church handshaking, kissing, bunny-hugging and generally swamping their fellow creatures in a deluge of Peace.

Of course, I exaggerate. But, being English to the umpteenth degree, I have to express a certain distaste for intense public exhibitions of emotion, especially when they are laid on to order. I cannot really take them seriously, any more than could the jolly old lady I met after this particular performance.

With a beaming smile, she said, 'I have to confess that I am not at peace when I feel I've been assaulted.'

It is rather naughty to laugh at a ceremony that means so well and was inaugurated with such good intention. And I ought to be ashamed of a sense of humour that delights in the presumably apocryphal tale of the man who, filled with love and compassion for his fellows, went the whole length of his church to embrace with the peace a poor lonely miserable individual, only to be told to 'get stuffed'.

I do not know who started it all, nor why it gets such a boost from the ASB.[1] Some say it was a mediaeval revival. I first met it several years ago.

I presume it was introduced to counteract the previous image of a church congregation being so many individuals or small groups scattered over the building keeping themselves to themselves. Is it a reminder that we are, in theory, 'members one of another'? If it is, I am, alas, one who finds it fails to hit the target.

Then Cedric reminds me that, although I do like to be regarded as 'somebody', I am far from being 'everybody', and tastes and opinions differ quite fairly on different matters. I must not expect everyone to share my lack of enthusiasm for this manufactured Peace; and if some – or even most – find that the practice warms the cockles of their hearts towards possible unknown neighbours, who am I to deny them such comradely spirit?

I merely ask them to be strictly honest about it.

For I did meet a lady who visited a strange church and received the full treatment during the service, only to be completely ignored by everyone at the coffee and bun session following.

Nor am I entirely sympathetic with the good woman who was viciously critical of her vicar's personal character but who conjured up a loving smile to accompany the standard words of peace at the Eucharist, only to continue tearing him to shreds afterwards.

Peace on the face does not go happily with war in the heart.

On the other hand, I heard one good man explain that the handshake is akin to the hand of healing and he feels he is administering a blessing. And very nice too but I wonder how many can view it that way. For myself, I can only think of offering my hands in that way at a healing service, but I may well see the light of day. I pass on the idea for consideration.

Meanwhile, Cedric reminds me that it is the Peace of the Lord we are supposed to be distributing and this is a necessary ingredient of loving our neighbours.

---

[1] The Alternative Service Book

Epilogue

When I was a child, I thought as a child (like Saint Paul) and took it for granted that I would be successful – and possibly famous – when I grew up. I had no vision of the necessary steps to achieve these desirable objects. If I thought out the details at all I supposed that my natural abilities and sterling worth would guarantee the reward.

When I became a man, I put away childish things, or some of them. One of them was the desire to be famous. This was not, of course, because I did not think I deserved fame but because of all the dreadful things that may happen to the famous, viz.:

1. You will be plagued by people who just want to tell others they have met you.
2. You may suffer from media hounds who are out to scavenge anything discreditable they may hope to find in your public or private life.
3. Someone else might write your biography.

The best answer to this last is to write your own, in some form or another and these pages are vignettes from my time as the fictional vicar of the fictional village of Chilford. I hope you follow the reasoning.

Any book needs a title, preferably one that has some connection with the contents of the book. It might be *A Highland Journal* (Queen Victoria) or *Scenes of an Uneventful Life* (any Tom, Dick, Harry, Lucy, Margaret or Melanie Jane) who wishes the great British public to know how important they really are.

Not having been involved in murder, arson, nor the kind of sensationalism that provides copy for a modern novel, I must look further than events for a title.

I am reminded of J B Morton's definition of an autobiography as 'a book of gossip about other people', and there is substance in that. His wonderful character Lady Cabstanleigh once thought of entitling her memoirs *Stray Bats from my Belfry*.

On the same principle I think I might simply call mine *Bonkers*, but this hardly does justice to a loving God who has so often saved me from the just results of my follies and little madnesses.

I think I will stick to *As Sheep among Wolves* when I write my memoirs as a parish priest and to trust Cedric to avoid the laws of libel.

I, of course, am the sheep, and it would be great fun to have a bash at Mr Demos. Nevertheless, it is the personal character of the victim that a biographer is really interested in, and readers of these pages might have observed a touch of cynicism in my make-up.

The disadvantage of being a cynic is that one is not believed when one is being desperately serious. So I hope other cynics will believe me when I say that I am a deeply committed Christian, by which I mean that my outlook on life is built on a personal relationship with the risen Lord Jesus, and that my whole philosophy is founded on the acceptance of the Bible as the inspired word of God.

Cedric then says that he appreciates that striving after Christian perfection is a lifelong job but he does think that I might devote a little less of my attention to the follies of sinful men and women and a little more to the forces at work combating them. It is, he says, very naughty indeed to dwell on the machinations of the devil while playing lightly on the victorious love of the Creator.

I wish Cedric would stop moralising. It tends to be most uncomfortable.

I retain my vision of what Chilford church might become: a community united in their devotion to God and to neighbourly care of their fellow men and women and all this in an atmosphere of love, joy and peace.

There is excellent material there, even if we have some way to go. And the Lord is wonderfully merciful and patient with his wandering sheep, not to mention the wolves. And, in spite of clever persons who insist to the contrary, he can still perform miracles.

I have just reread Isaiah 11:6 ('the wolf shall dwell with the lamb') and a little more in the same strain.

I know the context is 'God's holy mountain' but why should not Chilford have an allotment there? Then Mr Demos and I could sit down together as real buddies, working together for the good of the Church and parish without sniping at each other all the time.

That will be the day!